The Freak Table

By Gavin Hignight

ISBN 978-0-9814746-1-8

This book is dedicated
to those I have lost,
both living and dead.

Special Thanks to:

Brandon Auman
Rhianne Paz Bergado
Caleb Braaten
Ejen Chuang
Denette Clift
Spencer Cross
Sara Crowe
Brandise Danesewich
Audrey Evans
Tina Berger Everroad
Joe Gordon
Greg Hignight
Mae Ho
L Spencer Humphrey
Amanda Jones
Mike Kiley
Nicole Kiley
Melanie Lambert
Juliet Landau
Mike Lewelling
Jose Macasocol Jr
Del Martin
Cara Muerte
Robert Newman
Opee Patzkowsky
Kevin Ream
Duke Rojas
Frank Romero
Jeremy Ross
Gaby Ruiz
Alex Schultz
Casandra Shell
Ann Song
Jennifer Thompson
Tim Vargo
Kyle Von Vonderen
Deveril Weekes
Jenn Wexler
Jonny "2 Bags" Wickersham
David Willis

Also a very big thanks to the 100's of Freaks who banded together
to support this novel on Facebook.
Every single one of you helped make this happen.

Chapter 1: Orange Soda Rockets

A nd then it happened... Something hard struck me in the chest, pinning me up against the chain-link fence. There was a sting as I felt a second fist hit my chest. I realized what was happening when I saw an older kid in a sports jersey punching my friend Wes hard in the stomach. Wes curled over, fighting for air.

"You a pussy skater?"

I'll never forget those words.

Wes's eyes were tearing up from pain and the lack of air. I could tell he was having trouble breathing. I was so busy watching them that for a moment I forgot a big jock guy had me pinned up against the fence.

"What, you can't fucking hear me! You a pussy skater?"

I didn't know what to say. He punched me really hard in the stomach while hands from people I couldn't see held tight to my arms and shoulders. I didn't know what was going on, how we'd gotten into it or how to get out of it, so I answered him. As I spoke, I could feel their hands digging into my arms and the chain links pressing into my back.

"Yeah. I skate."

A look of panic shot across Wes's face. As I was contemplating how I'd probably said the wrong thing, a fist slammed into my face. I was stunned from the blow, so when the hands let go, my legs didn't work below me. I slumped to the ground, unable to even open my eyes against the smarting pain in my face. I could hear someone mutter "pussy skaters" as they walked away.

Then the sounds of the rollercoaster rocking on its tracks and the other sounds of the amusement park flooded back to me. My face was stinging and something thick and wet was dripping down my face. It was the end of summer; the night air coming down off the Rocky

Mountains was crisp and people just yards away from us were still having fun.

Little did I know that earlier in the summer when I started hanging around with Wes, the new kid in the neighborhood, and picking up skateboarding, this would be the way things were gonna go from now on.

Before that summer, I had been pretty much invisible. You could say I kept a low profile... Actually, I didn't keep a profile at all. Back in elementary school, I was just one of those kids who blended in. I was quiet, did what I was told, turned in my assignments on time, didn't get picked on with the slow kids, but wasn't one of the popular kids, either. I did the same things all the other kids were doing, which was being a kid.

I was so busy doing kid stuff that I guess I really didn't realize just how much I didn't fit in. The few times I did open my mouth in front of the other kids, I usually embarrassed myself or quickly proved to them just how much I wasn't like them. While the other boys were playing sports, talking big about the Broncos and John Elway or showing off to the girls at recess, I was most likely off somewhere pretending to pilot *Voltron* or fight crime with *The A Team*.

Most of junior high was actually spent at home with a "sore throat," "fever" or "the plague" —whatever it took. I hated going to school. More and more I felt like the other kids didn't understand me and I sure couldn't relate to them. I'd rather just have been at home watching *I Love Lucy*, *Wild Wild West*, or *Bewitched*. My poor attendance led to bad grades, and the bad grades led me into classes with the most dysfunctional kids at school.

As far as extracurriculars went, I didn't want to sign up for football or soccer, I didn't want to join a *team*. I didn't want to be in a club or on a committee. I felt lucky to make it through the day, so why would I want to do anything to cause me to be there later? School just wasn't where my life was taking place.

I liked staying up late on Friday nights to watch *The Twilight Zone* or some old scary bad movie. I was happy daydreaming and doing my own thing. As I navigated junior high, the other kids got louder and more annoying, and I retreated further and further into fantasy books, cartoon shows, or movies on cable—anything that had as little to do with school as possible.

My parents were pretty cool. A lot of kids hate their parents and always have problems at home. Not me. Maybe that's part of the reason I never fit in with the other kids at school… I wasn't dysfunctional enough. I was, of course, dysfunctional in my own way. By the time I was ready to leave junior high, the quiet kid who always blended in had been replaced by a skinny, awkward one who didn't want to fit in at all.

My dad was a master carpenter. He spent all of his life doing the hard work, and was now in a position to tell the men working with him what to do. We weren't rich, but we weren't poor either. My dad was working-class; he grew up poor and did his best to make sure I wouldn't have to know what it was like for him when he was a kid. He was kind of old-fashioned but never really pressured me to be one way or another. He just expected me to do the right thing and "keep my ass outta trouble."

My mom was a product of the 1970s. She was entering a strange place about the time I finished junior high. After a decade where she felt comfortable being a housewife and a mother, she wanted more. So she took a job, not really for the need of money but more for the need of something to do. Maybe it was because I was getting older, who knew?

We didn't have much family around. Both of my parents grew up in the south and moved away from their families. Colorado wasn't that far from Texas on a map, but in the way we lived our lives they couldn't have seemed farther apart. I don't think my parents could relate much to the rest of the family so we didn't see them much, just road-trips in the summer to the grandparents and holiday dinner visits from the one uncle who happened to live near us.

It really felt like a new chapter of my life was starting during that summer between junior high and high school. My mom was off working, I was getting ready for a new school, and I had a new friend I was hanging out with.

Wes had just moved into the neighborhood and I was the first kid he met. He was a *skater*, something that was mostly unknown to me. I had seen a couple of kids around who looked like him, with the bangs and baggy pants, but I didn't really know what they were all about.

Wes had come skating up the sidewalk one day and asked me if there were any other skaters around or where he could buy sex wax. I sure didn't know any skaters and I definitely didn't know what "sex wax" was. I didn't know what it was used for or where you could get it but I made a mental note to find out later.

I shrugged, embarrassed that I had no idea what he was talking about.

He laughed, saying, "Surfers use it on their boards but you can use it on your trucks or on curbs and shit so you can pull off tricks."

"I don't think there are any skaters around," I said.

He didn't look disappointed. Instead his face lit up a bit. "I have an old deck you could use. It's pretty thrashed, but it's better than nothing."

And that was that. Right then and there something changed. Something took hold and it would set me on a course I'd never come back from.

I spent the next couple months learning to skate, trying to pull off tricks, taking falls, wiping out and as Wes would say, "eating shit." I didn't have to be good at it to enjoy it, but the more Wes and I went out and skated, the better I got, or at least the better I became at falling and not completely killing myself.

And I quickly had a new bible. It was called *Thrasher* magazine. I would buy one when I had the money, or hang out in the grocery store and read one while my mom shopped. I'd stare at the pictures of real guys pulling off insane tricks and I'd fantasize about getting my hands on the skate decks, clothes, trucks, wheels, or stickers I saw in the back of the mag.

In the few short months between junior high and high school, I had found an entire new world. And I was determined to transform myself...at least as much as my parents would let me.

Fast forward to the end of summer. To think, moments ago Wes and I had been having a great time like all the other people there. We'd been celebrating one of our last nights of freedom before school and rushing through Lakeside Amusement Park looking for a couple of waver girls Wes had spotted. And then this...

I was on the ground clutching my sore face. I glanced up at Wes; he was looking down at me with a worried expression on his face while he held his side.

"Dude, there's a lot of blood all over your face. It's on your clothes, too."

It didn't hurt that bad. I'd already taken worse tumbles off my board in the past couple weeks. I was more concerned about telling my mom and dad where the blood on my shirt came from.

We stood there for a second. I couldn't believe what had just happened; it was like a real fight. Wes said it wasn't a fight—he said we got jumped because there were more of them than us. Having moved here from California, and being the guy who introduced me to skate culture, Wes always seemed to know more about things, so I took his word for it. We got jumped.

He was pissed.

"I can't believe we got caught off guard like that!"

He walked me over to a funnel cake stand—I guess I wasn't acting very normal. He wanted to try and get something to help clean the blood off my face and some ice for my nose. The ladies working at the stand gave us dirty, anxious looks through the slot in the glass. Through my watery eyes, I took notice of the graffiti scratched into the glass and how the florescent lights illuminated the interior of the stand. While I was marveling at that, Wes got even more pissed.

"You can't even give us some ice?"

They stared at him through the glass.

"My friend just got jumped! Would you please give us a rag or something?"

They went back to cleaning and acted like they couldn't hear him.

"Can you at least give me some napkins or paper towels!?"
A small hand reluctantly clutching some napkins reached through the window slot. The woman stared at me through the glass while Wes grabbed the napkins. She didn't say a word.

We didn't talk about what happened on the way home, and we actually never told anybody about it. We decided it was something that his parents and my parents didn't need to know.

Wes's dad dropped me off in front of my house. As I was climbing out, Wes gave me a firm look.

"I'll call you tomorrow, man," he said, and they drove off.

Luckily, when I got inside, the house was already dark. My parents must have already been upstairs watching the news. It was their nightly ritual and my lucky break that I didn't have to explain the shirt! I'd just bury it out in the trash can on trash day or something.

Lately, I'd been going out to my driveway and skating around at night before I went to bed, but after what happened earlier I was now second-guessing that. Who knew who might be driving by? I was wary of getting jumped again.

Instead of skating, I sat in my driveway watching cars drive by and looking up to the sky for satellites. I kept thinking about the exact moment when we'd been caught off guard, when we'd been in the wrong place at the wrong time. I kept playing it over in my mind, wondering if there was something I could have done differently— when I suddenly remembered something. We never even got to find those girls we were chasing after!

A couple days later I'd already forgotten about the siege at the amusement park. I had something new to worry about. I was just about to start high school. *A new school*, with new people, new girls, and who knew what else?

This was my chance. A fresh start. It was like my school career before this had been a drawing on an Etch A Sketch, and I now had the chance to erase every prior humiliation with a good shake. I could erase that I was the kid in class who said that he liked Phil Collins when everybody else liked Poison. I could erase that my mother enrolled me in tap dancing because she wanted a young Fred Astaire in the family. Now that I had a clean slate, maybe I could find more of my own kind. Whatever that kind was…

I had to get new school clothes and school supplies. My mom approved of my choice of Chuck Taylors for shoes. I guess the price agreed with her. Otherwise it was the standard new pair of jeans and a couple T-shirts. Nothing cool on the T-shirts, either—everywhere my mom wanted to shop had lame t-shirts.

I already had a cool backpack that this kid from down the street left at my house once. He was this stoner named Ryan and was always getting into trouble. The backpack had all of these patches on it like Iron Maiden and W.A.S.P. I didn't listen to either of these bands, but I liked the backpack. One day, Ryan had used the backpack to bring some Hot Wheels and firecrackers over to my house and he never came back for it. Then he just kind of disappeared from the neighborhood. Maybe he got sent off to private school or juvenile hall or something?

I really wanted to cut my hair before school. I wanted something that matched the way I was feeling, something new, new and extreme—not as extreme as Wes's hair, with the shaved sides and bangs that hung over his eyes, but something better than the standard Boy Scout hairdo I'd had my whole life. My father and I seldom got into fights, but when I told him what I wanted to do with my hair, he got pissed.

"I'm not gonna have a son of mine making a target of himself and walking around like a freak!"

When I continued to push, he got even angrier and said he'd ground me or kick me out of the house or make me wear a bag over my head, so I had to drop the debate.

Those last few summer days, Wes and I sat around on our boards and talked a lot when we got too tired to skate or it was too hot. The concrete would make now familiar noises under the wheels of our boards.

Everything we talked about seemed so important. We would talk and listen intently, really respecting where the other was coming from. He seemed like he had seen so much already, it made me feel kind of embarrassed about my own experiences or lack of them. But he didn't care or see it that way. It was nice to have a friend like that.

A couple nights before school was about to start, we were sitting in the parking lot of the grocery store. It was late and we were having another one of those talks. I think both of us were anxious about school coming up, but chose not to show it.

"I wonder what kind of girls are gonna be at the school? Were there any cool girls at your junior high?" Wes asked me.

"Not really. Unless we had a group project or something, I never even talked to the girls that much."

"I hope there's some waver chicks, like those two girls we saw at Lakeside. That'd be awesome!"

"Those girls were awesome. Why do people call 'em wavers? Their hair?"

"No, the music they listen to."

"Oh?"

A car squealed by and someone threw an empty can at us from the open window. It rattled as it bounced across the concrete. It didn't land anywhere near us, so we just laughed. Then Wes got quiet and looked around at the parking lot.

"Things were different back in California, man, things were different," Wes muttered, still looking around. I could tell he was still pissed about being jumped.

"Back where I came from everybody skates and everybody else is cool with it."

I told him how in junior high everyone treated each other like crap regardless of who they were, skater or not.

"If they're gonna be assholes no matter what we do, we might as well do what we want," I said.

Wes agreed, "Yeah, might as well give 'em one more reason, right?"

Two-liter bottles of generic soda were on sale real cheap at the grocery store. We were so thirsty we bought two each. Clearly we didn't need four liters of soda, so we each took our extra bottle and shook it up as much as we could. We shook like human paint mixers, putting our whole bodies into it. People driving by probably thought we were having fits.

When we thought the bottles were gonna burst from all of the pressure, we tossed them down cap first. They both shot up in the air like rockets. Orange soda sprayed everywhere as the bottles flew up into the sky. Mine veered off into the dark somewhere and Wes's landed on the roof of the grocery store. We were laughing so hard we could barely skate off when somebody from the store got pissed and came out yelling. It was great.

Chapter 2: The Freak Table

I thought my first day in high school would be like this big epic adventure, or like one of the many John Hughes movies I'd seen. But, the truth is that it was uneventful. It was actually kind of a drag. Somehow, Wes and I hadn't ended up in any of the same classes.

My poor attendance in junior high had come back to haunt me. I had gotten good grades on the work I did, but my overall grades were bad since I missed class all the time. So they placed me in the "at risk" classes. The rejects. I was now mixed in with all the hoodlums and kids who were short a chromosome. "At risk" of what? That's what I wanted to know.

The first couple of weeks of school were pretty lonely, especially at lunch. Wes and I didn't even have the same lunch period. I saw some cool-looking kids around—some skaters and some waver types. But since none of them had ever seen me before, I didn't get any notice or respect from them. I could tell it was a tight crowd.

My school was filled with the usual mix of kids that every school has. Preps, jocks, drama club kids, suburban wanna-be gangsters, stoners, religious kids, and those who wanted to be in student government. None of which described me. I didn't want to be any of those people or be doing any of those things. I just wanted to hang out and skate. If I wasn't doing that, I wanted to hang out with other people who did.

The dying breed at my school was the stoners. They were all juniors and seniors, a couple years older than me. They all had long hair, ripped jeans, and denim coats covered in band patches. They never wanted to hang out with anyone else, but they never really had a problem with anyone, either. A couple of them told me my backpack was cool once, but other than that they never really took notice of me. They were always drunk and stoned, always standing out in the smoking area telling tall tales about encounters with the cops or parties they had been to.

The jocks were the real problem. My dad always said it was because they were insecure. I guess that makes some sense, but hell, I was insecure, and I wasn't trying to beat the crap out of anybody. I guess that's how you can tell someone cool from someone who's a dick.

There was one jock who I got to know very quickly. Brad Thompson. He was a real dick. He was on the football team. He wasn't one of the biggest guys on the team but he was bigger than me.

We had history class together. The class was called "Great Leaders." I actually liked the class until he and his friends started messing with me. They all sat together in an idiotic hulking mass across the room from me. To make matters worse, there were also some cheerleaders in class. That makes for a bad situation. It's like combining two chemicals and watching them explode. Once those jock guys decided they wanted to show off to the girls, they needed a victim. I was the minority, so I was the perfect choice.

It started when we were covering Teddy Roosevelt. Brad and one of his footballish friends started talking louder than usual.

"Pussy skater."

"What a faggot!"

"We should kick his ass!"

I was fairly certain I was the "pussy skater" and "faggot" they were referring to. My skin started feeling hot and I was getting nervous, but I tried to act like I couldn't hear them. They continued speaking like this until class ended. "Fag." "Pussy." "Ass kicking." "Kick his ass." "Freak." "Faggot."

With those words fresh in my head, I left class as quickly as I could, knowing that I needed to find an ally fast! Where was Wes? As I scanned the book-carrying and backpack-clad bodies of the hallway, Brad caught up to me. Once we were standing face-to-face, I realized he was definitely much bigger than me.

"What did you say back in class?" he asked in his best tough-guy voice.

The truth was that he actually had a high-pitched sort of little girl voice, thanks to the cruelness of puberty. I didn't think this was the best time to inform him of it. But I did totally picture him taking steroids for football like a kid in an after school special or anti-drug filmstrip.

"I didn't say anything in class."

I didn't know what else to say. I was kind of caught off guard.

"Someone said you were talking shit, you pussy skater."

"I don't even talk to anyone in that class!" I said.

This was getting awkward. People were stopping to watch and I was getting that hot feeling under my skin again.

"Everyone thinks you're a fag, skater!"

I stood silently, without a response. As I tried to think up a come back, I realized a couple of the cheerleaders, along with one of his friends, were now watching. There was glee on their faces. Glee and anticipation. Where was that other friend of his anyway? There were three of them in class...

"You better watch it or you're gonna get your ass kicked."

I made the mistake of trying to reason with him.

"I didn't say one word in class today, so how could I talk shit about you? I don't even *know* you." As I contemplated the hint of desperation in my words, he shoved me really hard. It was at that point I realized where his other friend was. Kneeling behind me, so I would fall over him onto my ass. And that's what happened, me tumbling over him and slamming to the ground. As my back hit the ground, books exploded from my hands, scattering across the floor. Applause and laughter erupted. The gleam that I'd seen in the cheerleaders and his friend's eyes was now in his.

"Pussy skater!"

He and his friends walked away congratulating themselves. I sat up, rubbing my sore back. Once again, I was the one who'd been caught off guard. It was like the amusement park all over again. Only I knew I would see these guys again and again. Every day in the same classroom at the same time.

The next day I found FAG written on my locker in black Sharpie. I had a pretty good idea who did it, or at least which group did it. I was so nervous and so wound-up in class I didn't hear anything the teacher said. There was tension, muttering, snickering. How was I was supposed to be paying attention? I couldn't remember if we were still talking about Teddy Roosevelt or if we'd moved on to Franklin. Churchill on the offensive, Roosevelt on the offensive—hell, now I was on the offensive, too. I was now living in my own wartime.

After class, they followed me to my locker again. The entire time their comments sliced at my back, stinging my ears. *Just keep acting like you don't hear them; just keep acting like you don't know they're following you.* That was the only strategy I could arm myself with.

Just keep facing forward. Don't turn around.

As I got to my locker and fumbled with the combination, I could feel the burn of their eyes on my back.

A tap on my shoulder… I really didn't want to turn around. But I had no choice. I turned to find Brad his two friends. Behind them at a safe distance were the cheerleaders, of course.

"Why you keep looking at me in class, fag?" Brad preened in the spotlight.

"Don't you have anything to say, you fucking skater?"

As usual, I didn't know what to say.

"Why don't you chill out, man?"

The words just kind of fell out of my mouth

"Chill out, *please* chill out, you guys? I'm a fucking pussy skater," Brad squealed back.

I was really starting to get sick of hearing "pussy skater." He shoved me; the lockers gave a metal echo as I hit them. I could feel the bite of a combination-knob in my back.

"You better watch yourself, *skater.*"

I noticed not only the cheerleader girls watching in the distance this time, but also someone new. A skater guy I had seen around with short buzzed hair and a Dead Kennedy's shirt. He was watching nervously.

"What the fuck is going on!?" Wes walked up. He shot a dirty look at Brad and his goons. "There a fucking problem?"

"How nice. Your boyfriend's here to save you," Brad spouted off.

"Fuck you," Wes shot back at him.

Wes was more forward than I was. I envied that about him.

"What did you say?" one of Brad's thugs blurted out.

Just then, a teacher came out from behind the block of lockers. Had he been listening in the whole time? It was the shop teacher, Mr. James. He had a reputation for always looking like he was about to snap.

"What the hell's going on here?" he shouted at all of us. "Get to your damn classes!"

I loved it when teachers said things like "hell" and "damn." Mr. James had not only just saved us from a fistfight, but also lived up to his reputation. People around school said he was slightly disturbed because he was a Vietnam vet. There was even a story circulating about a time he'd had a flashback and snatched a power drill from an Asian student. Mr. James swore up and down that it was because the kid didn't have goggles on, but a lot of people said it was because he thought the kid was a Vietcong with a gun.

Crazy or not, he had broken things up just in time. Everyone scattered. The cheerleaders were the first to split, then Brad and his friends. I was left standing alone with Wes while Mr. James glared at us.

"What did you expect, looking the way you do, you little punks?" he barked at us. Not the reassuring words I was looking for out of a teacher.

"Get to class!"

With that he stormed off back toward the shop classrooms, muttering to himself. As Wes and I started walking away, the Dead Kennedys kid caught up to us.

"Those guys are real assholes, man," he said.

I turned around, surprised.

"Hey, I'm Phil," he said, reaching his hand out to shake. As I shook his hand, I glanced down and noticed he was wearing Vans. They were thrashed.

We introduced ourselves and then Wes had to split. Phil spoke up, looking nervously around.

"If that had turned into a fight, I *woulda* had your back!"

"Thanks," I said.

"We all gotta stick together, man. It's us versus the *mainstream.* They're right and we're the left, man." I liked the way he was talking—it sounded political and smart.

"Well, I gotta get to class. I'm always fucking late." And then he was off.

"Punch him right square in the nose," my dad said calmly, from behind the dim glow of his cigarette.

When I got up early the next morning to go to school, I found my dad where he could always be found at the crack of dawn: sitting in the dark, in his favorite chair in the den. He would sit there still as a stone every morning before anyone else was awake. No lights, no morning paper, no breakfast—just a cup of coffee and his cigarette.

I knew I could talk to him about what happened at school, but I hadn't wanted to say anything in front of my mom because she'd worry. Normally, I wouldn't have bothered his morning cigarette, but this had felt like as good a time as any.

"The next time he's mouthing off to you and trying to show off to his friends, just punch him in the nose. That will take the fight out of him."

The cigarette glowed red with another drag.

"That's how you deal with a bully. I had to deal with them when I was your age and the best way is getting right to it. Do you think they're gonna want to keep picking on you if they know they're getting a fight back in return?"

That was my father's brand of logic. Problem. Direct solution. Punch the guy in the face. He continued to tell me he didn't care if I got in trouble for fighting, if it meant I was standing up for myself.

He then told me the story of three goons who plagued him in his school days. For some reason, these guys didn't like him at all. All of them, including my dad, were on the football team. He said they would always hit him extra hard in practice and try to push him around. He wasn't specific about their names but he was adamant about the stupidity of one of them, who also happened to have a metal plate in his head for some reason or another.

Before my father had moved to Texas where he met my mom he grew up in a small poverty-stricken town in Oklahoma, so the visual he painted of this dull bully kid with a metal plate in his head was vivid, like a grotesque Norman Rockwell painting.

"I had to hit that guy as hard as I could right in the stomach, 'cause I knew it wouldn't do any good to hit him up top with that metal plate in his head," my father said with a proud, sly grin. Not an expression I often saw on his face.

"I hit that guy hard and he dropped! I got in a couple shots on the other two, they were bigger than me, mind you—then they roughed me up good. But you know something? After that day do you think they ever messed with me again? No! They went on picking on people who wouldn't fight back."

I thought about the story and what my dad had said as he gave me a ride to school that day. We talked about how soon I'd get my learner's permit and be able to drive myself, and about some yard-work he wanted to accomplish over the weekend.

He dropped me off in front of the school and drove away to some office or building his company was renovating. I was so relieved by everything he told me, I actually didn't mind walking into class. I was maybe even a little excited.

I wasn't a fighter by nature, but that day I was ready to lay into Brad if he started in on me again. I was ready. Any smart remarks and I was going to go off!

The teacher was lecturing and the class was busy taking notes. Instead of taking notes, I was face down in my notebook doodling pictures of guys falling off half-pipes. As I completed one with a broken leg, Brad and his friends made their move for the day. As always, it came without warning.

SMACK! Something damp and salty struck me in the face. A soggy fucking french fry from the school cafeteria. As it hit me in the face, the group chortled in hushed tones. The salt from the greasy fry stung at the edge of my eye.

"You fucker!" I shouted.

The class was now dead silent, all looking toward me in awe.

"Excuse me," blurted the teacher, "what did you just say in my classroom?"

As the teacher walked toward me, the group across the room erupted into full-fledged laughter. They were so proud. As the teacher shushed the class, she turned to me with a serious expression.

"What's going on here?"

I held up the undercooked french fry. "Someone threw this at me."

"It's still no excuse for that kind of language!" the teacher sternly told me. I could see Brad was smirking.

That was it. I was going to fucking knock him out.

"I don't want any further interruptions from you and I want to speak with you after class."

Brad and his goons continued snickering. The cheerleaders watched in eager silence. It felt like a hot eternity until class was let out and everyone filed out except for me. I heard their muffled conversations as they emptied into the hall. Brad had won again.

Once the room was empty, the teacher walked over to me and sat down. I didn't say anything. I didn't know what to say. I was so pissed. But I was also afraid of what was coming. The teacher started talking in a much calmer voice than I was expecting.

"It's funny. Most of these kids don't think I can see what's going on. They think they're so clever that I can't tell what's happening in *my own* classroom. It's not like this is my first year teaching... I didn't hold you after class to punish you. I figured you could use a break from all their bullying."

"It isn't *bullying*, besides, I was gonna deal with them," I said. I actually sounded like I meant it, too.

"And what good would that have done? You get into a fight and then you all get in trouble." I guess she had a point.

"I wanted to speak to you about something else."

I watched nervously as she walked over to her desk and dug around in a stack of papers. As she walked back, my eyes returned to staring a hole into the floor. When I glanced up, I saw her holding an essay I'd written on Thomas Jefferson in her hands.

"Did you notice when Brad and his friends started picking on you?"

I shrugged like I didn't know what she was talking about.

"I just figured they hate skaters. That seems to be going around at this school." The teacher chuckled. "Well, I don't really know anything about that. I think what it really comes down to is that you don't belong in these classes. It's been fairly obvious the last two weeks. I think Brad and his friends are jealous because you speak up, you know a lot of the answers, and have things to contribute to class discussions. They've done a good job of taking that away from you, because you've become increasingly quiet in the past few days."

She shook the essay in her hand. "This is written very well, and it's all the proof needed to move you into normal classes. If that's what you'd like, I'll talk to the principal and you'll be out of here."

For the first time, I realized the meaning of the saying, "The pen is mightier than the sword." How strange was that? Something I'd written was gonna get me out of there and away from them! I could switch classes and wouldn't have to deal with Brad anymore. Perfect.

"I'd love to switch into the other classes," I said in disbelief.

Later at the dinner table, my mom was very excited that I was going into "normal" classes. I could tell she was always worried about that kind of stuff.

My dad had a slightly different opinion.

"Son, I'm glad you got into the higher classes, but in some ways you're just running from your problems. Eventually, you'll probably have to deal with this Brad character. If not him, then you'll have to face another Brad somewhere else."

He might have been right, but I didn't care, I was just glad to escape from those assholes.

After dinner that night, I grabbed my board and met up with Wes at the grocery store parking lot. We tried to make a ramp out of some shipping crates we found in the loading dock behind the store. The ramp didn't work too well. Every time we hit, we were thrown off our boards. So we aimed the ramp into some grass and took turns launching ourselves into the air. I got a few grass burns when I hit the ground, but it was worth it.

Though we were already a few weeks into classes, going to school that next day was like walking into my very first day all over again. I started out the day with a lecture in the principal's office. His name was Mr. Yates and he was a bulldog of a man. He wasn't the largest guy, but he radiated authority. He looked professional, but also like he could kick some ass in a bar fight or something. He was telling me about the importance of sticking to my grades, proving myself, and how my workload would increase. But instead of really listening to him I was distracted thinking about him in the military or something, killing guys with his bare hands and smoking cigars and stuff.

The next stop was the counseling office. There I met Mr. Dorris. He happened to be assigned the portion of the alphabet that included my last name. He was a very nervous man, I thought to myself. He kept looking over the rims of his ancient eyeglasses like someone was out to get him. He also would only address me by my last name. I couldn't believe this man was advising anyone—he seemed so feeble and broken

I couldn't help thinking someone should be giving him guidance. Maybe it was because he had a woman's name for a last name? I bet he'd had his share of Brad Thompsons giving him shit for that when he was my age. Once he finally gave me my new schedule, I hurried off to my new classes.

Unfortunately, I got out of his office right in time for gym, which I knew even with the schedule change I would probably hate. We usually ended up having "team sports," which meant everyone crammed into the gym, all the jocks played basketball and everyone else painfully pretended to hustle back and fourth across the court. You had to keep on your toes, because the jocks would throw the ball as hard as they could at your face if you weren't paying attention.

If we weren't inside being forced to play basketball, we were outside being forced to run laps on the track. If we stopped running, the gym coach would shout at us.

"Hustle, hustle, hustle! Come on, you panty-waists!"

I hadn't even been in high school a month and I was sick and tired of hearing the coach say that. As hard as it was for me, I really felt bad for the fat kids. There are some kids who just aren't made for that kind of exercise. I was lucky I could at least fake it. But now I had to fake it in front of a completely new group of people. I had already gotten to experience the humiliation of being in the locker room with one group of people, and now with the schedule change I had to go through the whole process again.

As it turned out, I got a lucky break. Wes was in my gym class. So was that skater kid Phil who I had met the day before. He walked up wearing some really long shorts and a torn-up Teenage Mutant Ninja Turtles shirt.

"Hey, the coach said that any of us who weren't playing basketball had to go outside and run. You wanna go?"

I looked over toward Wes, who was already playing basketball with a bunch of those jock bastards. How he could stand those jerks was beyond me… I guess it was easier for him, since he was so athletic. He could hold his own with them in sports.

"Sure, anything to get out of here," I said, while contemplating Wes and his basketball game.

As we made our way outside to the track, Phil and a couple stoner guys kept looking back suspiciously. Then, out of nowhere, they took off running. Phil grabbed the shoulder of my shirt and pulled me along with him. I stumbled over my own two feet as we made our way to this concrete wall near the bleachers. As we dove behind the wall, Phil and the other two guys started laughing while trying to catch their breath.

"Damn, I thought he was gonna turn around and see us. Damn," Phil kept chuckling.

"Fuck running. We'll just hang out here for a while…" said one of the stoners as he lit up a cigarette.

"You guys ever get caught over here?" I asked.

He took a drag. "Fuck no. This is one of the safest spots in the school. I even heard that one French teacher, Lewbosky, comes out here to smoke pot."

I wasn't sure about his pot-smoking teacher legend, but was glad to get away from the labor camp running nonetheless. After class I couldn't find Wes for lunch. I know I must have missed him while avoiding the mandatory shower in the boys' locker room.

Not a fun activity, the mandatory shower. Unless you enjoy rowdy naked jock guys laughing and sliding across a shower room floor on their bare asses. It was like a game to them to see how far they could slide bareback. To me, the whole experience of the locker room was just plain disturbing. I didn't even like being around those people with their clothes on. And me alone, naked and vulnerable to attack… Fuck that.

I started off for another lunch on my own when Phil caught up to me in the hallway.

"What you doing for lunch, man?"

"Not much." I was clutching a book for homework and my brown paper bag, so the answer was painfully obvious.

"Come on with me, man. Now that we have the same lunch, you have to sit at the Freak Table with the rest of us." I wasn't sure what Phil meant by "Freak Table," but anything sounded better than another lunch by myself.

The cafeteria smelled the exact same way every day no matter what they were cooking. It was always the same smell, and not a pleasant one, either. The smell reminded me of getting slapped in the face with a soggy french fry. The commons area of our school was filled with a collection of folding tables. They were always stored there and unfolded for lunch. Off in one of the far corners was the Freak Table. Phil and I sat down with our lunches and I looked around at the scattered, odd little crew. He introduced me to the few he knew.

First was this guy named Rob. He looked preppy for a skater. His hair was neatly cut and non-descript—just brown, combed to the side and normal. He was wearing a large baggy T-shirt that read "MODE USA 1988" in large letters. He was also wearing some baggy cargo pants.

He reached his hand out. "Hey, man, how's it going?" He wasn't really interested in an answer. No sooner I replied than his face was back down in a book and his lunch. Maybe he was cramming for a test or something?

Next was a girl with long brown hair. She was wearing a black dress with a button that read "Meat is Murder." Her name was Sarah. As soon as she was distracted by a conversation with someone else, Phil leaned over and whispered to me.

"Dude, she's a little crazy. Her parents are really religious, so they're always mad at her over something. Even worse, I heard they're in the middle of a divorce."

I watched as she poked at her lunch and continued speaking to the girl next to her. She seemed nice enough. She talked through the whole lunch, on topics ranging from an assignment she didn't want to work on to how brilliant she thought *The Picture of Dorian Gray* was. I didn't even know who this Dorian Gray guy was.

Some time during lunch, another girl in black joined Sarah. Something about her almost looked like a grown-up or a professional businesswoman or something. Her name was Rachel. She was pretty, but was fixed up plainly. She looked remotely like Rob, which made sense when I found out he was her older brother.

"So I think we're gonna have another party," Rachel said to Sarah.

I couldn't help overhearing. Sarah glanced at me with a mind-your-own-business sort of look. I suddenly became totally engrossed with my lunch. Of course, I went on listening to them in their now slightly more hushed voices.

"You are *so* lucky. I can't believe how often your parents leave town! You and Rob have it made. I can't believe they never have anyone stay with you."

"Yeah, they're always going to all those trade shows or whatever it is they do."

"They leave town I swear, like, once a month."

"And they're always at some convention getting drunk as skunks."

The two girls giggled.

I snuck a look around at everyone else at the Freak Table. Some skater kids, a couple of wavers, some kids who didn't really fit in anywhere, and some leftover stoners. Everyone was relatively quiet and keeping a low profile until this loud kid walked up, slamming his lunch tray really hard on the table.

"They took my fucking board!" he shouted.

His name was Toad. The top of his head sported a short messy green sprout of hair. His clothes were more torn and mangled than anyone else's at the table. He was the most punk rock skater I had seen. And he was really pissed off.

"Fucking administration took my board! They said they *confiscated* it. And they said there's a new school rule that we're not allowed to bring our boards to school anymore. They said that it causes too much trouble!"

The table quickly erupted in outrage. Phil spoke out first. "What do they mean trouble?"

"These jocks were fucking with me because I rolled up to school on my board," said Toad, "so I got into it with them." I didn't doubt he *got into it* with them. I had the impression that he wasn't one to back down from a fight.

"The fucking principal stopped it and pulled *ME* into the office. Not them. Of course it was my fault, right? So I told him what happened and he said if it seems to be a source of trouble maybe we shouldn't skate to school. Then, he took it and said it was confiscated. Can you believe that shit?"

"Fuck that. They fuck with us and it's *our* fault," I said more to myself than to anyone at the table. The words just kind of escaped from my mouth. Toad took a good long look at me. He was silent as he sized me up.

"Who the fuck are you?" he said. "You look like a poser." The others at the table started laughing. I was feeling hot under the skin with embarrassment. It was just as I was thinking that I should get up and go off somewhere alone to finish my lunch when I heard Phil speak up for me.

"This guy's all right," Phil said.

"I haven't seen him around," snarked Toad.

"He just got moved from the other group of classes."

"I never seen him around skating before."

Toad turned to me; he squinted a little while he spoke and he continued to stare me right in the face.

"How high can you ollie?"

Everyone at the table looked at me. I could have told him about a foot and a half high. I could have told him two skate decks stacked on their side, I could have said six feet and he still wouldn't have been impressed. So I gave him an alternate reply.

"A hell of a lot higher than you, seeing as how I didn't get my board taken away by the principal." Everyone laughed. Instantly, I wanted to take it back. I was expecting a fist in my face when Toad started to laugh.

"You asshole!" he said, grinning to himself while patting me on the arm.

And that was that. My first lunch at the Freak Table.

Chapter 3: Art Class

The absolute best thing about being moved into the other classes was my art class. I don't think art was of much concern to my school district. Our art classroom was small and located in the basement of the school, looking more like a storage area than a classroom. It was taught by a post-hippie. But that didn't matter—what mattered was the girl in the next row.

Her name was Elizabeth. The first day I saw her, she was wearing black-and-white striped tights, a black skirt, and an INXS T-shirt. Her hair was light brown, cut at an angle, and slightly longer than most of the waver girl hair I had seen around so far. Her skin was fair and perfect. She was one of the most beautiful girls I had ever seen, the kind of girl that someone classy would refer to as "a lovely creature." Her expressions were generally a mix of pensive and brooding. She was something else…

I felt a rush whenever knew I was going to see her. Of course, it was seldom that she even glanced up from her notebook or assignment, so I had a feeling she didn't feel the same way. I wasn't even sure she knew I was there.

It didn't matter. This was now my favorite class for sure! I was much more comfortable with my new schedule and classes and *for a short period of time* loved going to my art class. I never got much finished because I was always distracted, but it was art class. It wasn't like I really had to do all that much anyway.

Instead of getting work done, I was busy building the fantasy of our long and fantastic high school romance, the tougher years when we fought to stay together in college, the storybook wedding, and the walks on the beach in our old age. Sadly, the only *real* interaction between us was her getting to watch me being ridiculed on a daily basis.

There were some factors I hadn't counted on when I made the foolish decision to inform my new friends at the Freak Table that I had a thing for the girl in my art class.

Over the past month, I'd gotten to know the members of the Freak Table better. They were becoming my friends. Well, some of them. Phil and I started hanging out and skating. Toad was in our grade but wasn't in any of our classes because he was in the "At Risk" program. I thought it was strange I hadn't seen him before, but then again, hearing how much he liked to ditch school, maybe it really wasn't that strange after all. Rachel and Sarah were a year older, which doesn't sound like much, but they reminded us at every opportunity that we were younger and less experienced. They really got a kick out of it; Phil said they were always like that to him. For "older and wiser" they sure did giggle a lot.

I had mentioned at lunch that I couldn't wait to get to my art class because of the girl I liked. I didn't realize she was Sarah's friend. I also didn't realize that Elizabeth was dating this preppy jock guy who sat directly behind us in art class.

His name was Chad. He was an even bigger, larger, dumber fucker than Brad. Great... I went from a *Brad* to a *Chad*. Were all these guys cranked out in a factory somewhere? A product line where generic assholes with blue jeans, baseball caps, and similar names were churned out? He wasn't as physically aggressive, but he was tormenting nonetheless. It was worse, actually... He had one more year of bully-experience than my previous adversary.

Of course, it eventually got back to him that I had a thing for Elizabeth. Sarah decided she had to tell Elizabeth about it almost as soon as it came out of my stupid mouth. It must have spread to Chad soon after. I pleaded with Sarah to keep quiet about what I'd said, especially after hearing just who it was that Elizabeth was dating. That preppy bastard...

I couldn't understand how Elizabeth was dating this guy. I wasn't sure I had ever even seen them talking in class. It amazed me that they could be dating. Didn't you have to talk to someone to be dating them? And didn't you have to have something in common? From where I was sitting, they had nothing in common. He was mainstream shit and she had good taste...at least in music and style, anyway. Maybe it was because he had money and was popular? I heard he sold weed to kids he knew, and that made him rich in both cash and friends. But did she buy into that? Did she really?

The exaggerated news of my "undying love" for this girl spread like a wildfire, and each gossipy, giggly girl in class was a twig ready to burst aflame. Chad sat directly behind me with some jock buddy of his. Elizabeth sat next to me on the right side and a mentally-challenged kid named David sat next to me on the left.

Art class became the new Great Leaders class. I was ridiculed thoroughly. They pulled shit every chance they got. Any joke that could be made at my expense was made; every time they could hang me out in front of Elizabeth, they would. I wanted to die every time I had to go to class. The tingle on the back of my neck, the embarrassment-burn under the skin—it was guaranteed in every class.

"Hey, you guys seem like a good couple."

"You guys should go out."

"Hey, Beth, I think that guy sitting next to you was just checking you out."

"I think he was trying to look down your shirt!"

Chad's words were laced with cockiness; the air was thick with it. His friend would snicker and laugh every time, even at jokes he'd heard before. They were both larger than me and they had a year of age on me, factors which combined to intimidate the hell out of me.

She would sit there silently, doing nothing except painting. She didn't even really paint. She would just stare down at her paper and swish around the watercolors, making a puddle that would eventually turn brown. The "special" kid next to me sat quietly and worked on his assignment. I envied that he was off in his own little world while I confronted this battlefield of insults. I would sit there angry as hell and not say a word. I didn't have the ammunition to fire back.

Elizabeth seemed to be absent a lot. After a while, I couldn't believe I was actually happy when she didn't show up. At least it meant I wouldn't be made a fool of in front of her. Not that they stopped on the days she was gone...

"Oh, Elizabeth's not here today. I wonder where she is?"

"Oh, she's at my house waiting in bed for me."

"That makes sense, she is *your* girlfriend."

"Yes, yes, she is my girlfriend and I'll go home and do her later."
And then snickering.

It got to a point where I would face nothing but the front of the class. I never turned my head, not even to the side. I felt if they saw the look on my face it would just give them satisfaction.

I couldn't help it; I really liked this girl for some reason. I didn't even know why. I didn't know what to do about it. And after everything, I didn't even want to but I did. And those assholes continuously tearing into me didn't help.

"Just leave it alone, man," Phil said. "It will pass."

We were in the back parking lot after school. Phil and I were walking home to grab our boards and go skate. I looked toward Rob and his sister Rachel. They were silently observing our conversation. They didn't say a word, but I'm sure they exchanged a look. The two never really said much to me unless I said something to them first. They were a tight-knit unit, reluctant to let anyone in.

Sarah climbed out of the backdoor of the Rob's car and walked over to me. I still really regretted opening my big mouth around her in the first place. And I really was growing to dislike her. I had no interest in talking to her at that point.

"Listen, Phil told me about those assholes in your class," she said. "If I would have known it would turn into something like this, I swear I wouldn't have said anything to anybody. I don't even like Chad."

I glanced up at her. She wasn't making eye contact. Neither was I, really. Instead I stared at her "Meat is Murder" button.

"It's cool, I guess. I just hate those guys," I said.

"Yeah, none of us really like them," she said.

They climbed into Rob's car and drove away. Phil and I continued toward home.

"At least she tried to apologize, man, you gotta give her that," Phil said. He was right, but I still wasn't sure I liked her much.

"Can you believe we have to leave our boards at home? We could be skating right now without that stupid 'no skateboard' rule!" I said, trying to change the subject.

"Yeah, you know what I think? I think they don't want us bringing our boards to school 'cause they hate skaters! They're afraid of us shredding the benches and shit!"

"Yeah," I agreed. Then a car full of jocks sped by, screaming some insult we couldn't understand and throwing a Slurpee at us. Dodging it successfully, we continued walking home.

Fall was in full swing. The air grew cooler, and the oranges, reds and blues of the sunsets were picturesque. Leaves changed colors and fell. All the yards in the neighborhood were covered in a blanket of leaves.

My birthday was coming up, my grades were okay, and I was getting to be a better skater. I hadn't seen Wes as much. To my amazement, he'd joined the basketball team. How he could stand to be around all those assholes was beyond me! Even worse than him joining that team was the fact that he had practice when we'd normally be skating. A lot of times I would meet up with Phil. Sometimes I would meet up with Toad but I could tell he didn't like me too much. He was always calling me a "poser" and a "fresh-cut." I didn't know what a "fresh-cut" was. But I could tell from his tone it wasn't exactly a compliment.

One night after school, Phil and I were pulling off tricks on Oakwood Drive when we had a run-in. The place was a block that Wes and I found that had a curb going off at an odd angle. It was perfect for rail slides and grinding. During the summer, Wes and I would always go there and he would try to show me how to rail slide without killing myself. By now I was pretty good at it.

A few of the jock guys from basketball practice were walking home and had decided to take Oakwood. This was bad news for Phil and I, as there were more of them than us and we couldn't clear out before they spotted us. Worse, one of them was Brad Thompson. Worse than that, Wes was walking with all of them.

Phil spotted them first. He turned to me panicked. "Dude, we should split."

I saw that Wes was with them and decided to have faith that everything would be fine.

"Look at those two faggots!" Brad yelled out. "You two on a date?" It was nice to see that Brad hadn't lost his charm since I'd seen him last.

"I haven't seen you since mommy pulled you out of class."

"Pussy!" someone from the group bellowed out. His friends laughed and Wes just looked down with a grim expression. I was stunned and disappointed. Why wasn't Wes saying anything? I thought if anyone would understand it would be him. More importantly, I thought we were friends.

I tried to break the tension.

"Hey, Wes. Check it out!" I got some speed on my board, hit the curb, and pulled off a rail slide.

"I've been working on it," I told him.

But I could tell he was embarrassed about it now.

"Cool, man," he said under his normal tone. Then he turned to the others. "Let's get going, guys."

He was blowing me off… He was blowing *me* off on Oakwood Drive.

"That was a cool trick," one of the faceless jocks said.

He walked toward me. "Mind if I try?" he asked, reaching his hand out for my board—well, the old board that Wes had loaned me. I looked at Wes. He shrugged. Then I looked at Phil. The look on his face was *get the hell out of here.* Then I looked over at Brad.

"Don't be a jerk. He's serious, let him try your board," Brad said.

"I don't know," I said.

"Come on, man. I just want to try that trick on the curb," he said. So I handed it over. It was Wes's board, after all, and I was hoping the gesture would smooth things over. As he took the board from me, the look in his eye turned from earnest to evil. He started laughing.

"Hey, Brad. You need a new skateboard?" he sneered while handing the board over.

Brad replied, "What would I need with a skateboard? I ain't no pussy skater."

"All right, give it back!" I said.

"Give back the board, man!" Phil shouted. He was now sounding more angry than panicked.

They started walking off. I followed, pushing Brad in the shoulder from behind. "I said, give it back. Now!"

One of Brad's friends shoved me back while Brad took the board and set it down on the ground. He put his foot on it. Wes finally spoke up.

"Just give it back to him, Brad."

"If he wants it, he can go get it," Brad said. Then with all of his might he pushed the board across the street with his foot. It rolled straight toward a sewer opening. I ran as fast as I could to grab it. I don't know if he planned for it to go down or not, but before I could reach it, my board shot right down into the sewer like billiard ball into a corner pocket. Screams of hilarity, surprise, and laughter bubbled up from the group of jocks.

"Dude, that's fucking harsh," I heard one of them say. Brad was looking over at me. I started to charge him, but one of his large friends caught me before I could get to him. I screamed, "You asshole!" Wes got into the middle of it all and pulled the mass of letter jackets off of me. He shouted over them and their laughter.

"Come on, guys. Let's go. Let's just fucking go!" They walked up the street, swaggering in victory.

I just stood there. I couldn't believe what had just happened. Again, my choice to be a skater had put me at odds with the people around me. I looked over at Phil, who was already at the opening of the sewer feebly trying to retrieve my board. I walked over and bent down next to him, looking inside. It looked dark and deep. Night was falling fast, which made it even harder to see down inside.

"I'm so sorry, man," Phil said. He looked like he really meant it. "I can't believe those fucking assholes. Assholes. Who do they think they are? Just because we go to a school where there're more of them than us. Fuck them. They're just jealous because they don't have enough balls. They just conform, man. They're fucking conformists. Dude, I'm sorry about your board—do you have another one, like an old deck or something?"

I was kind of embarrassed to admit that this wasn't even really my board.

"No," I said calmly. I was so angry.

Phil and I gave up on the search. Neither of us could lift the nearby manhole cover even when we pulled on it together. After trying a couple times, we sat down on the curb, defeated. We had one of those talks that just months before I would have had with Wes. We really bonded right there, at the spot where my board was swallowed up by the neighborhood. Phil told me stories of times he barely escaped attacks for being a skater. I told him about the amusement park incident and how Wes used to be a cool guy.

"Maybe he just got sick of dealing with it, so he sold out, man," Phil said.

Maybe Phil was right. Secretly, I felt like I really owed Wes for turning me onto the lifestyle, but I was also pissed at him for giving up on it. I really did love this. I really loved where I was going. I didn't care if the others thought I was a poser. I wasn't doing it for them. And I wasn't doing it for Wes. If he was gonna sell out, then fuck him.

Phil and I kept talking until way after dark. It was really starting to get chilly in that September-October sort of way. We talked about the people at school we disliked, the people we liked, the girls we were into. Everything.

"Man, girls always go for older guys, not younger ones," Phil said. "Especially hot ones, 'cause they can get older guys. They always go for the older guys who have money and can drive cars and shit."

He interrupted himself. "Wanna get going? I'm fucking freezing!"

"Yeah, guess we should go."

We started back toward home. I was now walking while Phil skated slowly beside me. Once we got to the block where we'd split up, Phil gave me a sober look.

"Hey, I'll see you tomorrow at hell—I mean, school."

I smiled. "Yeah. See you tomorrow, man."

I could hear the hiss of his skateboard wheels as he made his way down the street, fading into the dark. As I walked, I kept wondering how long it would be before I'd be making that noise again. I felt empty-handed as I entered the house. I'd been setting the board next to the front door, like a raincoat, and now it was gone. I hoped my parents wouldn't notice because I didn't want to alarm my mom or give my dad the impression that I wasn't standing up for myself. I quietly went upstairs for a while and listened to The Dead Milkman cassette that I had borrowed from Phil. I sang along to the line, "Fucked up world, we're all veterans of a fucked up world." That song cheered me up. I thought to myself that tomorrow would be another day so I went downstairs and ate dinner in front of the TV and called it a night.

I was lying in bed, getting ready to go to sleep, when I had an idea. It was a great idea. Those jock bastards had taken away my board. They kept trying over and over again to take away who I was. I wasn't going to let them get away with it; well, at least I was going to express myself no matter what they did to stop me. My thoughts and my master plan were interrupted when the phone rang out in the hallway. It was unusual for us to get calls this late. My mom came in.

"Wes is on the phone," she said. I reluctantly got up and answered the phone.

"Yeah, what?"

"Hey, it's Wes. Sorry about today, man. That wasn't cool."

"Yeah, it sure wasn't. What do you want?"

"I'm trying to make things cool, man."

"Why? You seem to be doing fine with your locker room buddies."

(a pause)

"Things are just different here, man."

"Yeah, they are. You sold out and now I'm a *pussy skater.*"

"That was my old board anyway, man! Not like you lost any money on it!"

"You want me to pay you back for it or something? Guess I was in the wrong place at the wrong time, huh?"

"No, that's stupid, man! If you want, you can use my other board. I'm not going to be using it during basketball season."

"No thanks. I'd hate feeling like I owe you anything. Your jock friends may not like that."

"They're not all bad guys."

"They're a bunch of pricks."

"You don't even know those guys."

"Yeah, too bad. Guess I'll see you around."

And I hung up the phone. I guess I hadn't realized my anger toward him until I'd heard his voice. I was more pissed at him than anything else. I felt like he had really backed out on me. My mom came into the hall as I was heading back to my room.

"Everything okay?" she asked. I tried to give her a reassuring look.

"Everything's fine," I said. "Just dealing with some jerks at school."

"When I was in school, there just weren't all these problems," she said, with frustration. I didn't have a response. I wanted to say something witty to reassure her, but I didn't. Instead I said nothing. I just shrugged, went back into my room, played more Dead Milkmen, and went to sleep.

I woke up an hour early the next day. It was time to put into action my brilliant plan from the night before. I went into the bathroom and made some adjustments to my appearance. I grabbed my father's clippers and gave myself a sort of haircut. I shaved and cut and got rid of chunks at a time, leaving the top long. Then I went downstairs and grabbed my baseball cap and my infamous rock-and-roll patch backpack. As I was getting ready to leave, I came across my father, who was sitting in his chair in the dark, as usual. A stream of smoke wafted off of his cigarette.

"You put away my razor when you were finished with it?" Crap. I didn't realize he'd known I was up there.

"Yeah, I didn't mess it up or anything."

He leaned into the light.

"Let me see the damage," he said calmly.

I took off my hat. He looked pissed. "You're making yourself a target. I shouldn't let you go to school looking like that."

"I don't feel like them. I don't belong with them. I don't want to look like them! They know it, and I know it!"

"When you get home tonight we're going to the mall and getting rid of that mess. I don't want my son walking around looking like a menace."

He didn't understand that I was trying to make a stand in my own way. I didn't know how to explain it to him, either.

"Why isn't your skateboard in the hall?" he said, while still glaring at the top of my head.

"It was Wes's board and he wanted it back, I guess."

My father nodded.

"Get on to school before your mother sees your head and has a fit."

I nodded and said goodbye. He said goodbye, too. That was one of the cool things about my dad. He could really be pissed at you and still have enough class to say goodbye, and mean it.

I got to school and found someone had placed a Pixies sticker on my locker over where FAG had been written earlier. I didn't really know that band, but it looked a hell of a lot better on my locker than the crude-fag-graffiti. Now I'd just have to wait for the administration to yell at me for putting a sticker on my locker. It was strictly forbidden.

Luckily, I hadn't seen Wes at all. Not even in the locker room. Maybe he was avoiding me. I didn't care; it was better than running into him. Once lunch was over, I had a favor to ask of Phil.

"You have pretty good handwriting, right, Phil? I mean, it's pretty legible, right?"

"Sure, why?" he asked, puzzled.

I revealed a black Sharpie that I had taken from the junk drawer at my house. "I just need you to write something so it can be read really easily," I told him.

Carefully, Phil wrote what I had requested on the back of my head while we both tried not to laugh too hard and mess it up. Before we knew it, it was time to go and I was on my way to art class.

I walked in and Elizabeth was already sitting at her desk. She was leaning over her assignment and looking beautiful, as usual. A couple strands of her hair had fallen down, hanging in front of her face as she studied her work. She barely even glanced up when I sat down.

Roll was called and Chad and his prick friend weren't there. I couldn't believe I was finally ready for them and they hadn't show up. That just sucked. I figured I'd get to work on my assignment. We were supposed to copy something in the style of Georgia O'Keefe. You wouldn't think painting a big flower on your paper would be that hard, but mine looked like crap.

Halfway through class, Chad and his friend came in. They were loud and obnoxious coming through the door. They gave the teacher some line about being held late in student government. But most of the class knew by their watery eyes and tardiness they were most likely high.

In a rare occurrence, Elizabeth actually turned around and exchanged an odd look with him as he sat down. Before they even got their work out, they started making fun of me. I allowed them to for a while.

"Maybe next year when you hit puberty you can ask Elizabeth out. I'm sure she'd be game, bro."

"When do little girls hit puberty?"

After that round of snickering, I'd had enough. I calmly removed my baseball cap and set it down on the desk. The snickers behind me vanished, replaced by silence.

Where all my hair was shaved off on the back of my head, I'd had Phil write **FUCK YOU** in big black bold letters. It was probably his best penmanship.

The silence was broken by raucous laughter. I couldn't tell if Chad was impressed or pissed. He just kept laughing like he couldn't believe it. The teacher got up from her desk and came over.

"What's so funny that it's causing you to disturb my class, Mr. Edwards?"

He pointed to the back of my head. The teacher still hadn't seen what I had written on it. He made eye contact with me, then looked back at the teacher.

"Look at his haircut!" he said.

I couldn't believe he hadn't rat me out… But why?

"Put your cap back on," the teacher said. She looked at the group of us.

"I don't want to hear another sound from this part of the room. Am I understood?"

Everyone nodded yes, and turned their attention back to their work. I looked over and exchanged a brief but odd look with Elizabeth. She looked almost as annoyed as the teacher.

I finally had a victory over those two jerks behind me. I felt like I had finally stood up for myself. The feeling didn't last long. Chad and his buddy caught up to me in the hallway right after class. It was just like with Brad back in Great Leaders class. The factory that cranks these assholes out must train them to find guys like me *after* class. That's why he hadn't said anything to the teacher. He wanted to save me for himself.

The metal locker felt cold and hard as I slammed up against it. I turned as fast as I could so I'd at least be facing them. Using the advantage of his size, Chad shoved me again, and I flew backward into the lockers. The feeling of the combination locks digging into my back was getting way too familiar.

"Pretty fucking funny," Chad said as he pinned me. His friend was in my face. "You can't just tell someone to fuck off and not back it up!" His size and strength were so fucking frustrating.

I just stared at him. Then I blurted something out.

"I'm sick of your big fucking mouth every day! I didn't know you were dating Elizabeth. I don't even know Elizabeth. It's not a fucking problem, so why don't you leave me alone!" The look on his face held both surprise and amusement. He laughed.

"Fair enough. You gotta get better at standing up for yourself, man," he said in a fucked-up big brotherly tone. He still held my shirt collar tightly. Then I heard her voice. Why did I have to hear her voice? Why did she have to see any of this?

"What are you doing? Just let him go, he's harmless," Elizabeth said.

I had never even heard her speak that clearly. It might have been the first time I'd really heard her even speak and she'd said…harmless. Did she really just call me "harmless"? She sounded like she was referring to someone's pet hamster.

Harmless? I had to do something. I broke my arm free of Chad's hold and punched as hard as I could toward his face. I didn't hit his nose, but I sent him staggering back. I must have caught him off guard. As quickly as I could, I lunged toward his friend with my fist, but before I could make contact I was sacked from the side. It was Chad. He'd recovered from my punch a little faster than I'd hoped. I hit the lockers with a clang as Chad pressed up against me. Screams of excitement filled the hall from the gathering crowd.

Chad's friend laughed. I squirmed away from Chad's hold and lunged for him again. This time I knocked right into him with my whole body. Then I felt a punch hit my side really solidly. It stung. I kicked behind me really hard. I think I hit something because he backed off some.

As I turned, a teacher and a janitor came to break us up. The two of them took hold of me. I looked up to see Chad's always-perfect hair was messed up. At least I'd messed up his hair. The crowd hissed in disappointment that their entertainment had ended. There were tons of people gathered around, but from what I could tell Elizabeth was not one of them.

I didn't get detention, which I couldn't believe. It was my first trip to the principal's office for disciplinary action and the visit had me a little surprised. I did get quite the lecture, though.

"I'm sure your parents wouldn't approve of what you've written there on the back of your head."

He stared me in the eyes, waiting for me to show some sign that I understood what he was talking about. Sheepishly I nodded, then looked back to the floor.

"You're new here, so I'm gonna give you a break. This is your 'Get out of jail free' card," he said. "You're using it up on this little head-graffiti stunt. Got it?"

I nodded.

"I'm still going to have to tell your parents about the fight." I nodded my head yes, like I understood. He got up from his chair, came over, and sat on his desk in front of me. I felt like he was looking right through me.

"You've got to find a better way of dealing with your problems. If these guys are harassing you, tell me. I'll deal with them. That's my job, not your job. Got it?"

I nodded my head yes. He had already talked to them before I'd been brought in, so I didn't know what they had told him. All I knew was that it was already an hour past school letting out and I was itching to get away.

"Now, I talked to the other two. They admitted they'd been giving you a pretty hard time and probably had it coming. They said they'd lay off. If I hear of any more trouble from them or you, you're going to see I'm not always a nice guy. Got it?"

I nodded my head yes.

"Your father is on his way to pick you up. Do us both a favor and go wash that off the back of your head before he gets here."

"Yes, sir," I said.

He laughed. "You don't have to call me 'sir,' just call me Mr. Yates and keep your ass out of trouble." He pointed to the door. I marched straight to the bathroom, ready to scrub.

I had to wait outside the front doors of the school while my father talked privately with the principal in the doorway. It was making me nervous until I heard what I thought might be a chuckle from one of them. I distracted myself by keeping my balance while walking on the edge of one of the planters out front. I almost fell off when my dad came outside.

"Let's go," he said in a firm voice.

I was silent as I climbed into the passenger seat of his old truck. He didn't start the truck. Shit. I was really gonna get it. With a sigh, he turned and gave me a look.

"Did you mess up your clothes any? You tear 'em up or anything?" he asked.

"Just my shirt. Not too bad, though."

He started the car and we pulled out of the parking lot. He turned on the headlights.

"You get any of them good? Bust their noses or anything?"

"No, but I did good. They didn't beat me up."

"It's probably best you didn't do too much damage. We don't want any lawsuits. Everybody's always suing these days."

I was silent the rest of the drive home. I looked at the windows and porch lights of the houses we passed. I wondered if the people in those houses had days like I'd had today.

As we pulled onto our street, my father broke the silence.

"We'll just tell your mother you were standing up for yourself so she won't worry about anything."

"Thanks," I said. "I don't want her to get mad or anything."

When we got into the house, my dad had me go in and change my shirt. Then he told me to get my mother so we could all drive over to the mall. He said he needed to pick something up, but I could tell that he really didn't need anything. He normally hated going to the mall, so I could tell it was just his way of trying to make everything okay after a long day.

We ate dinner in the food court. They had Chinese and I had pizza. Afterward, they went to a couple of department stores looking for undershirts or something boring and I went to the music store and thumbed through countless albums and cassettes. I kept studying album covers, keeping my eye out for bands that I thought I'd like. After the mall, we stopped by the skate shop and I went in and looked around while my parents waited in the truck. As I was drooling over the skate decks on the wall, the guy from the shop walked over to me.

"Here, man. Take a few of these, for you and your friends."

He handed me a few stickers with the shop's logo. They were cool and I thought I'd better make sure to save one in case I ever got another skateboard.

Crammed in the truck with my parents, clutching my new stickers, and listening to some AM talk radio station my father had on, I couldn't help but think about what an okay night it turned out to be.

Just a few hours before, I'd been thinking it was the end of me. Funny how things work out sometimes.

Chapter 4: Operation: Squareback

"**D**ude, you fucking rule! I heard you took on two guys at once!" Phil was ecstatic. "Rachel went to go meet up with Elizabeth and saw the whole thing! Those assholes."

"I heard you got your ass kicked, you fuckin' skater," a stoner from the Freak Table muttered from behind his bangs. He wasn't trying to be a dick; it was just the way those guys were. Phil wouldn't let the moment be ruined. He continued to tell me all the different things people were saying.

Toad sat down at the table. He looked irritable as usual until he flashed me a wide grin.

"You fucking idiot. You got in a fight with the one preppy I don't totally fucking hate. If he gets kicked out of school for fighting, who the hell am I going to buy my pot from?" He continued to smile. I hoped that he wasn't really mad. I couldn't tell.

Rachel and Rob sat down. Up until that point, they'd been friendly but not personable. Rachel waited a few moments before speaking. "So, I saw your little show yesterday in the hallway."

I didn't know what to say. I should have kept feeling proud but the look on her face deflated me for some reason. "Elizabeth is so annoyed. She thinks you got into it with them just to try to impress her. She thinks the whole thing is juvenile of all of you."

I couldn't believe it. She thought I was juvenile? Me? After sitting in that classroom and listening to her jackass "boyfriend" carry on for the past month and I'm the juvenile one? Is that what Elizabeth sounded like? Great.

Angry and without the words to justify myself, I looked down at my plate and the cafeteria spaghetti in the shape of an ice cream scoop.

"I think it's awesome," a voice called out.

It was Rob. "Everyone's always going on about what a cool guy Chad is and he's a fucking prick. People just like him because he's got money and throws those big house parties on Snob Hill and gets everyone all high."

Rob reached over to shake my hand.

"It's about time someone went swinging after that guy."

"You just don't like him because people think he has better parties than us," Rachel said coldly, over her salad. Where did she get a salad? Not in this place.

"Listen, I could care less about that guy's parties. The kind of people he invites and the kind of people we invite—let's just agree, they're two different worlds!"

"Yeah, ours are way better!"

"Think about it for a minute, look at me right in the face, and tell me you don't think that guy's an asshole," Rob said to Rachel. There was tension. Sibling versus sibling. Discomfort at the table grew as he continued to stare her down.

"You're right. He is kind of a prick," she laughed, and their argument was over just like that. Rob turned back over to me. "We're gonna have a great party soon. You'll have to come by."

That was it. That was the invite in. They were finally claiming me as one of their own. I was actually invited to one of their events. I finally had some allies, or at the very least, maybe I belonged to something. Toad looked over while slowly spitting a clump of half-chewed green beans through his teeth.

"I still think you suck for punching my drug dealer."

A couple weeks had passed since the art class incident. The two behind me moved on to making fun of other people in the class. Elizabeth was showing up less and less. She never seemed to be in class. When she was there she was just silent and focused. She never looked over in my direction. Nevertheless, I couldn't help being intrigued by her. I would glance at her out of the corner of my eye, trying to figure out what was going on in that head of hers.

Wes and I didn't even bother acknowledging each other in the halls anymore. Sometimes it was awkward, but I really didn't care. Phil and I were already good friends and since the "art class freak out" I was hanging around more with Rob, Rachel, Sarah, and Toad.

I still couldn't skate after school due to the Oakwood sewer skateboard incident. It still really pissed me off. One day, I found a cartoon on a sheet of notebook paper stuffed into my locker. It depicted my skateboard calling for help from the sewer.

Phil and I were sitting around outside at The Slab. The Slab was a concrete area outside the school that was designated for smoking, it looked like the place where prisoners in jail would be lifting weights and having meetings about whom to shiv next. There were all kinds of kids huddled around in small packs sharing smokes; the last remaining stoners, the few jocks who actually admitted they smoked and a couple of the cowboy kids. The cowboy kids were more of a minority than us! Although The Slab was filled with older kids and many rough faces we didn't recognize it was the only other safe haven for the dregs of society such as ourselves at the school.

Phil was telling a story about the day before. He had skated to the skate shop to rent *The Search for Animal Chin*. This was the Holy Grail of home videos for us; we had read about it in *Thrasher* but none of us had seen it yet. Any of the skate videos we could get our hands on were links to a distant world of others who understood us. We could watch the pros, our heroes, or pick up tricks, or watch some amazing wipeouts.

The skate shop that gave me the stickers was the only place in town that rented skate videos. There was no reason to even bother looking anywhere else.

"So I was skating through the mall parking lot on my way home when a car full of these jock guys started honking and calling me a pussy skater, right?"

Phil had our total attention.

"So I flipped 'em off, and they tore out of the parking space and drove around the corner the wrong way of the traffic to come after me!"

"You flipped them off?" I asked, both shocked and impressed.

"Their car was facing the other way—I didn't think they could do anything!" He continued, "So I skated off as fast as I could. I was kicking faster than I ever have. I was thinking, 'Fuck, I gotta get out of here!' So I jumped off my board and started cutting through yards and over medians. Luckily, they were stuck to roads, 'cause of their car."

"What kind of car were they driving?" I asked in amazement, not wanting to miss one single detail of his survival story.

"It was a square-back, packed with fucking jock guys, man! I didn't know how many there were, but they meant business, so I cut through this field, which gave me some time. I ran like hell! I ended up in that new housing development over by the mall, man. There was no one around! I thought if they caught me, they were gonna kill me!"

Phil looked around. Now almost everyone on The Slab was listening to his story.

"I heard their car coming around the block—you know how those Volkswagens sound—so I dove into the basement window of one of those unfinished houses. I wasn't sure if they saw me duck in there or not. I was freaking terrified, man. I could hear the Volkswagen engine slowly coming up the block. It passed by a couple of times. I just kept ducking down and nearly shitting myself. I guess they got tired of looking for me 'cause they finally drove off."

"That's a hell of a story."

"You're lucky you got away!"

He shrugged with a prideful smirk on his face.

"How's the video?" I asked.

His expression turned to one of concern. "That's the worst part. I don't know why, but I panicked and left it there in the window-well. I thought if they caught me, they'd take it and trash it or something. So now I have to go by after school and get it. If I don't get it back to the skate shop, they're gonna charge me like eighty bucks! I never even got to watch it!"

"I'll go with you to get it," I told him.

"Good, I didn't want to go alone in case those guys were driving around again."

Phil and I made plans to go down and find it after school. We figured we'd try to watch it before he returned it to the store. Phil was worried some construction worker found it and kept it, thinking it was a porno or something. We decided we should get Toad to go with us to find the tape. If we got into some kind of trouble, Toad was the guy to have around.

Just as we were getting ready to leave the sanctuary of The Slab to go find Toad, Rob walked up to us with a big smile on his face. He held a piece of paper discretely.

"There you guys are. What's going on?" Before we could even answer, he interrupted us by handing the paper to Phil. "It's going on tonight, guys. We're having a party and you better be there."

Phil looked around at the various shady faces around us, then discretely unfolded the small flyer. It was a photocopied cartoon of Rob and Rachel with Xs for eyes and beers in each hand.

"Great flyer!"

Rob nodded. "Yeah, I work in the counseling office, so I can use their copying machine. Don't let anyone see this, all right? We don't want it getting busted before we even start." The idea of having a party and making flyers for it seemed brilliant to Phil and I.

"Are your parents out of town or something?" I asked.

"Yep, some kind of conference. I'll see you guys there tonight, right?"

We nodded our heads yes.

"Good. Feel free to bring whatever you want. We'll have stuff there but you never can have too much. I've got to go give these to a few more people." With that, Rob was off. Phil and I were pretty excited. It was Friday and we finally had something cool to do.

Once we got back inside the school, Rob and Rachel's party was the only topic of conversation amongst the Freaks.

"Hey, Sarah, are you going to Rob's party tonight?" Phil asked.

She gave him a withering look.

"Yes, I'm going to *Rachel's* party tonight." She followed up by giving *me* a strange look. She then looked back over to Elizabeth and Rachel, who were across the hall coming toward us.

"You know who won't be at the party tonight?" she asked me in whisper. I shrugged. I didn't know what the hell she was talking about. "That jock bastard who Elizabeth was dating. They finally broke up."

I tried to contain the message of pure joy that was probably written all over my face.

"Good, we don't need any jock bastards there anyway," I said, still trying to maintain a poker face.

"What do you think about that?" she asked me. I was starting to realize how much she loved gossip. I had a safe answer.

"I really don't know what to think of it." Once in a blue moon, I actually said the right thing. It shut her up.

"Okay. Well, see you guys tonight." She walked over to join the other girls.

Phil turned to me. "Don't you think she's hot?"

He was into Sarah.

"Man, she's so awesome. I heard she even lived in Europe when she was a kid. I wonder if she ever got to see The Cure?"

To two kids living in the suburbs of Denver, a girl who had been to Europe was about as exotic as it got.

"She was probably too young to go see The Cure," I said.

The bell rang for class and I was saved from having to continue the conversation. Phil and I agreed to meet up after school and go straight to the housing development to retrieve *The Search for Animal Chin*.

Even though I had just seen her in the hallway Elizabeth wasn't in art class again. I guess she was ditching since she didn't want to see Chad. While he and his friend made barfing noises and giggled to themselves I sat there worrying that she wouldn't be at the party later. The party! I couldn't stop thinking about it. What a cool night it was going to be ahead, first we'd embark on our covert mission to retrieve the lost tape then we'd go to the party.

It took us a while, but we figured out the military time was 1600. We were off on our mission, walking cautiously from house to house, careful to keep checking behind us for surprise attacks and ahead of us for places to duck and cover in case the square-back returned. We were just about to reach the target, making our way as silently as possible. The tape was almost in our hands…

"You guys are fucking pussies!" Toad shouted at the top of his lungs. "If those guys were driving around yesterday, there's no reason they'd be around here today. Get over it!"

Maybe Toad had a point? Maybe we had psyched ourselves out a little. But it was kind of fun. When those assholes chased you and you got away or barely escaped it was fun in a screwed-up sort of way.

We found the tape! It didn't look like anyone had bothered with it or even knew it was there. We sped off to Phil's house to watch it. Cutting through a field on the way, we passed an old blood-stained mattress on the ground.

"You know what that mattress is for, right?" Toad asked us with a sinister look on his face. "Vampires live down in that hole over there and use the mattress to drink blood from virgins."

Toad continued with his story and assured us of the credible source that had informed him. I'm not sure if it was because of our good mood or because it was so close to Halloween, but we chose to believe him and got the hell out of there before sunset. By the time Toad switched his story from vampires to a serial killer, we were already at Phil's house.

Phil lived with his mom and stepfather. He had an older sister but she was off at college somewhere. He told us that his sister was pretty cool and was always getting him into cool bands that no one had heard of. She turned him onto Oingo Boingo; he said his first concert was Oingo Boingo and the Red Hot Chili Peppers. That got me to wondering what my first concert would be.

The house was kind of messy. There was a picture of Elvis painted on velvet sitting on the floor of the den. Phil told us his stepfather had bought it at a garage sale and his mom wouldn't let him hang it, so it just sat there.

Phil's stepfather walked in the door as we were finishing the video. He wore the remnants of a suit and tie, and had a tired expression on his face.

"What's goin' on, girls?" he asked.

We all shrugged like we didn't know he was talking to us. Then I could tell by the panicked look on Phil's face that we'd forgotten something. We'd been going to grab some of his stepfather's beer from the fridge before he got home. We lost track of time watching the video! Stricken, I looked over at Toad. He, Phil, and I were thinking the same thing… How were we going to sneak out some beer?

We'd decided earlier that if we just took a couple from each of our houses, no one would notice. I had never been drunk before and was looking forward to it. Phil had lots of stories about his adventures with beer. Toad also had stories of adventures with beer, as well as vodka, whiskey, gin, and pot.

Phil and I tried to distract his stepfather while Toad went out and probed through the refrigerator in the garage for beer. We asked him about his day at work. We could tell he really didn't want to talk about it. He just kept saying, "TGIF fellas, TGIF. Do yourselves a favor, never grow up and get a freaking job in an office."

He continued his lecture about working for shitty jobs until a loud **BANG** and rattle came from the garage. He looked straight at Phil.

"What's your hoodlum friend doing out in the garage? Is he stealing my tools or something?" he asked with a smirk on his face.

"No, he's a…"

I interrupted, since Phil wasn't doing the greatest job.

"He's trying to find a flashlight," I said. Phil's stepfather slowly got up. We didn't know what to do.

"Isn't there one in the kitchen?" Phil asked. His stepfather started walking toward the kitchen. "Tell him to come on in and I'll get him the flashlight from the kitchen. Phil, you know where the freaking flashlight is. What, do you guys like sending him on wild goose chases or something?"

As he left the room chuckling, Toad rushed back in. His duffle bag was loaded with what looked like the majority of a twelve pack.

Phil cringed. "What the hell are you thinking? We said two or three! He's gonna kill me."

Toad shrugged. "What? He had a million out there. Dude, he won't notice."

"Hide 'em, hide 'em, here he comes," Phil barked at Toad. I almost started laughing when Phil's stepdad came in the room because I knew how guilty we must have looked. He handed the flashlight to Toad.

"What's this for?" Toad asked.

Crap. That had to be it for us.

"I thought you needed to borrow a flashlight, Toad!" Phil barked out.

"Oh, oh yeah. This'll work, thanks."

"So what are you guys up to?" Phil's stepdad asked. "Watching a video?"

"Yeah," Phil replied, "skate video I rented yesterday." His stepdad started toward the garage. "Plug it in so I can check it out. First I need a fucking beer."

As Phil's stepfather went into the garage, we figured our luck couldn't last. I gave Phil a look of silent panic. Phil gave Toad a look of anger and Toad gave us both looks of guilt, denial, and defiance.

"Phil!" We heard his stepfather call from the garage as he entered the room holding a couple of beers. We were dead.

"If you guys don't mind hanging out a bit while I watch the video, you can split this beer between the three of you." He held up the can.

"One beer between the three of us?" Toad asked, almost offended. Phil's stepdad replied, "Take it from me, Toad. If you're gonna have a drink *you have to learn to pace yourself*. And another thing," he said, pointing at the top of Toad's head, "never get a haircut after you've been drinking!"

As we all laughed at Toad I couldn't help thinking we had gotten away with murder...

Chapter 5: The Sweater Party

The sun was down, the streetlights were on, and Phil had just finished berating Toad for his beer thievery as I came out of my house to join them. The entire walk from Phil's place, Toad had just kept saying, "Dude, later on you'll thank me for it."

My parents didn't really drink, so there was no beer in my house. I did take what was left of an old bottle of whiskey from a cabinet in the garage. I'm pretty sure it was a leftover from a raging party in the '70s or something. Although boring now, my parents had partied before I was born; I'd seen pictures. My dad used to have a big moustache and they both had embarrassing clothes.

To no real surprise, there was no beer to be raided at Toad's house. His place looked like something out of *The Day After*. It was a disaster. Phil and I wanted to get out of there as quickly as possible because of the screaming kids and an equally loud screaming mother. As we walked out of Toad's driveway, he pulled a beer out of the duffle bag and cracked it open.

"What? I need to unwind. You see what I have to live with in there?"

I guess he had a point. We did make him duck into some bushes to drink it, though. Phil and I were terrified of someone driving by and busting us.

"You guys are total pussies, man," Toad told us with contempt as he chugged down the beer. I think if they made a talking Toad doll it would say, "You guys are pussies" when you pulled the string.

On the way to Rob and Rachel's house, we took a slight detour to look through the dumpsters behind the grocery store. Wes and I had discovered during the summer that the newsstand in the plaza sometimes threw out old porno mags there. No luck on our search, but we did find some old rotten tomatoes, which exploded quite well when thrown against the wall. Some guy came out the back door to have a cigarette and nearly had a hernia when he saw us.

"Hey! Hey, you!" he shouted as his cigarette fell out of his mouth. We could barely run away we were laughing so hard. Phil kept yelling at Toad not to shake up the duffle bag of beer.

We got over to Rob and Rachel's about nine-thirty. There were already a few people hanging out at the house. Rob was busy instructing them to move their cars. "Listen, nobody park in front of the house." Someone booed. "Park down the block so we don't draw any attention to the house or the party, all right?"

Rachel was in the kitchen, playing bartender. They had recently discovered Everclear and managed to include it in everything they were concocting.

Their house was really nice. It was in a neighborhood pretty far from mine, so it took us forever to get there. All of the houses on their block were huge and had two stories and multi-car garages. It was a contrast, to say the least, from where we had just been. Toad's house could probably fit into Rob and Rachel's garage.

The place was fixed up in an attractive way and everything inside looked expensive. Some people have houses that looked "lived in" and others have houses that look just like the ones you see in magazines. Rob and Rachel's was somewhere in between. They had cleaned the place and turned off certain lights strategically to give the party some mood.

I just kind of hung out between the kitchen and the room where everyone was. A wallflower-type position that I was afraid I'd occupy at every party I went to for the rest of my life. I sipped on a warm beer, which I wasn't enjoying. It had been hours since we removed it from Phil's refrigerator. The beers must have been shaken up when we ran from the guy at the grocery store because the first one Phil opened exploded all over him. He was pissed because Sarah had just come to the party and saw it happen. I thought it was funny. Also, I didn't mind so much that Sarah had just walked in because Elizabeth was with her.

When they walked in, something snatched the breath out of my lungs. The room slowed down for a brief second; everything became warm and limitless for a moment. She didn't see me, but I saw her—beautiful, and almost fragile.

I had never seen her outside of school and it was kind of surreal. She wore more make-up than she did in school, a lot of black around the eyes. She was wearing a long black skirt and a military dress jacket with a t-shirt. Her t-shirt read "Concert: New Order" in neon letters. I tried to play it cool, acting like I didn't see them walk in. Instead, I pretended I was busy laughing at Phil and the exploding beer. I don't think he appreciated this.

The party was underway. It didn't take long for it to fill up with all kinds of people. The crowd was mostly wavers and punks. They all seemed older. I didn't recognize many of them. Rob told me that a lot of the people there used to hang out at some club that got shut down and that was how they all knew each other. I heard some of them also went to the community college nearby.

People kept changing the music and getting in disagreements about what should be played. Every now and then you'd hear a drink get dropped, followed by laughter and cheers. Toad was drunk off his ass. He seemed to be a pro at this. He was out in the backyard trying to ollie on a deck that had no trucks or wheels on it. Good thing there was grass because he kept falling down and eating shit. He was really having a good time.

Phil could be found within a given radius of wherever Sarah was. They were already friends, so I don't think it seemed awkward to anyone but me. I made the rounds through every room, acting like I was looking for someone. Whenever possible, I would try to figure out where Elizabeth was hanging out. She had been in the kitchen for a while making what looked like one badass drink. She must have emptied an entire bottle of rum into her coke.

I ended up talking to these guys from some other school for a while. They had safety pin piercings, and black motorcycle jackets. One of their jackets was cool—it had a painting of the Joker on the back, laughing and holding a camera. As the guy was telling me how he painted the jacket himself, Elizabeth entered the room, talking to some girl with jet-black hair that was teased and ratty. That ended up being the same moment when this guy named Terry came in. He was loud and obnoxious. As he joined the other two I was talking to, he shot me a foul look.

"Hey, man, who's this poser?" he said, pointing at me.

I was feeling warm under the skin with embarrassment. Great fucking timing. Those kinds of guys acted like they came out of the womb wearing liberty spikes and leather jackets. I dreaded what would come out of his mouth next.

Instead, he patted me on the shoulder and blurted over and over again, "Just fucking with you, man! Hey, where's the beer?" He stumbled off. I glanced over to see if Elizabeth had heard any of that exchange. She was gone again.

Peering into the other room, I saw her. She was sitting on the floor in front of the TV, a drink in one hand a worn-out yellow legal pad in the other. She was staring at the TV with the same intense gaze that she would give her artwork in class. I walked in to see what she was watching. It turned out the room was empty except for her. All of a sudden, it was just Elizabeth and me. There was a music video on the TV.

"I absolutely love this video," she said, not looking away from the screen. "I love this band and I love Martin Gore." Those were the first words she had ever spoken to me. I wasn't sure what she meant. I wasn't sure who Martin Gore was, but she'd spoken to me and that was a start. I looked down at the list in front of her. It was full of song titles, names of bands, and numbers.

"What's the list for?" I asked. She looked up at me almost as if she didn't realize there was anyone else in the room with her.

"It's what's on the tape. Have you ever seen *120 Minutes*? Robbie and Rachel and I have been recording all of the good videos off it. We watch it every Sunday night and record what's good."

She went back to staring at the screen.

"What's playing right now?" I asked. She laughed. "It's Depeche Mode! They're one of the best bands ever. You should really listen to them."

"I'll have to check them out," I said. I wish I could have thought of something clever to say. I looked at the TV again. Elizabeth began rewinding the tape.

"What are you doing?"

"I'm rewinding it," she said. "I *must* see Martin again." This was amazing. She and I were talking. It was just us—the party wasn't going on around us, the people weren't making noise, and the world didn't matter. I finally had a moment with just Elizabeth. And she was being civil. Of course, it was too good to last and had to be interrupted. Toad came crashing into the room with Sarah and Rachel.

"Did you know there's something called a Vita-Course out there behind the house? There are soccer fields and some bleachers. We have to go raise some hell!" Toad exclaimed.

"I see you found the tape," Rachel said, looking at me. Then she looked at Elizabeth. "Did you see all of the awesome stuff we got last week?" Elizabeth nodded yes.

Sarah with her big mouth had to make the moment awkward.

"We interrupt anything?" she asked with a grin.

Elizabeth was quick to reply. "No. I need a refill." She spilled some of her drink as she got up and moved toward the other room.

"Are we going to go check out the Vita-Course?" she said while swaying.

Rachel carefully picked up the yellow notepad from the floor and turned off the TV. The party was getting out of control. Noise. Trash. People. Booze. Everywhere. Rachel, Elizabeth, Toad, Phil, Sarah, and a few other people I didn't know all agreed to jump the fence and explore the dark park and soccer fields. Before we left, I grabbed my jacket and Rachel grabbed what she called her "Morrissey sweater."

One by one we dropped over the wooden fence, each time with a light thud. Since Phil was slightly drunk, he got a few splinters in his hand going over. A couple of guys I didn't know brought a large jug of cheap wine. It was pretty funny watching them pass it over the fence. The group of us walked into the dark, away from the noise of the party. It took time for our eyes to adjust from the light of the party to the dark of night. I was worried I was going to step in a foxhole or something and really embarrass myself. We walked in smaller groups now, talking amongst ourselves. I never seemed to be in a group that was talking with Elizabeth, though.

The Vita-Course was some kind of fitness park. It had a concrete path that led through a path of pre-designed exercise stops. You would jog a little ways, stop, do some sit-ups, then keep jogging. In the middle was a bunch of soccer fields. At that moment, it was completely empty and silent. Whoever designed it didn't bother to put in lights, so it was like this big black void that existed just beyond the rich people's houses.

The nighttime breeze was chilly in a perfect way. I could feel the night and the fall air all around us. The ground was soft and the air smelled crisp and fresh. We swung up and down on a soccer goal post until Toad accidentally bent it. We laughed when he hit the ground. Even Toad was laughing.

Rachel kind of fell on the ground because she was tipsy, so the rest of us just sat down around her. She was going on and on about her Morrissey sweater. It was a cardigan style and she kept swinging it open on one side and talking about how Morrissey opened his sweater the same way in one of the videos she recorded.

"This is the best party we've thrown. And this is my favorite sweater! You know why?" Rachel asked drunkenly. "Because it's my Morrissey sweater and I can swing it open like this." She swung it open yet again. "From now on, everyone who comes to our parties has to wear sweaters like this and they have to learn to open them like Morrissey! If they don't, they have to leave. And that's that. If you can't, then you're not welcome at the Sweater Party!"

Everyone laughed.

"What?" Rachel asked.

"The Sweater Party?" Elizabeth asked.

I'll never forget the way her voice sounded when she spoke. I'll never forget the way the moon illuminated her pale face. She was beautiful sitting there in the dark.

One of the punk guys held out the almost-empty wine jug to Rachel. "Maybe you need some more to drink," he snickered. Everyone laughed.

There we were. We were with friends. We were free from all of the bullshit.

Phil sat on the ground while Sarah tried to find the splinter in his hand. I'm sure he was enjoying the hell out of it. The two punk guys continued drinking their wine. Toad and this other guy kept running by and kicking an imaginary ball into the bent soccer goal. Elizabeth sat on the ground staring off into the night while Rachel continued on and on about the simple beauty of the Sweater Party. The stars were up above us and I didn't think that life could be more uncomplicated or magical than at that moment. I didn't want it to end.

We got up and started doing this thing that Toad showed us. He said he had learned it in a pit at a show he'd been to.

"You hold the right hand of someone and they hold your right hand. You do the same with your left hands, crossed under the right, and you pull on each other and swing as hard as you can in circles," Toad said excitedly. "It's a good way to knock a lot of fucking people down when you're in a pit!"

There was no pit. Not even music. But we all spun around multiple times, except for Sarah and Elizabeth, who were both too drunk to do it without puking. I actually thought I was going to puke after doing it because Rachel wouldn't let go. She just kept laughing and pulling harder backward as we spun. Then we crashed down on the ground. The stars up above me were all warped and I had trouble catching my breath because I was laughing so hard. After we recovered, we got up, brushed ourselves off, and started back to the house.

The mood was completely different when we got back. We climbed onto an old crate to scale the fence and dropped down to find the backyard empty. As we got into the house, we saw people picking up their stuff and quickly clearing out. Some drunk stoner guy clutching a bottle of Jack passed us.

"What's going on?" Rachel asked, while looking at the mess.

"Fucking cops on their way. Somebody pissed off one of the neighbors."

"Shit," Sarah said. "We gotta get out of here! Beth, get your stuff. Let's go!"

Underage punks, wavers, and weirdos tried to escape in a drunken exodus. Rob came back in through the front door. He looked exasperated.

"We gotta get everybody OUT NOW and turn off all of the lights. We should probably split for a while, too," he said.

"What happened?" Rachel asked.

"Some asshole named Terry climbed onto the neighbor's Jag and pissed on the windshield. Then he fell down with his dick hanging out and set off the car alarm!"

I started laughing. So did Phil. We were met quickly with dirty looks from Rachel and Rob, who rushed back outside in crisis mode. Sarah stumbled over, grabbing her keys and her coat. "Elizabeth, we have to go!" She was obviously still drunk.

"You can't drive like that. You're smashed," Phil said. I nodded in agreement.

"We can't wait around here and get busted by the cops," she said.

She had a point. I could hear sirens in the distance. "We're outta here. We'll be fine."

They went outside. Phil and I followed. In all the chaos, I couldn't see where Toad had ended up. Phil and I caught up to Sarah and Elizabeth as they got to the car.

"You're too fucking loaded!" Phil pleaded with her. She seemed way more willing to drive drunk than deal with getting in trouble with the cops.

"I'll drive," I said.

Sarah laughed. "You're a fucking freshman. You can't drive."

"I have my permit and I'm totally sober." I glanced at Elizabeth, then back at Sarah. "I'd feel bad if anything happened to you two."

"He's right. He's just about to get his license. Let's just get a few blocks from here at least!" Phil agreed.

The girls looked at each other; I could tell they didn't want to do it. I could also tell that Sarah's drunkenness was hindering her decision-making process.

"Okay, here!" She slapped the keys into my hand. A few seconds later, we were off. I just hoped to get out of sight before the cops arrived.

I had only driven the truck my dad had been teaching me on, so this was a lot different. I asked them to keep the stereo down, which annoyed them, but I was nervous as hell. Phil sat shotgun and the two very drunk girls were in the back. Sarah kept complaining that I needed to hurry up because she was feeling sick.

I kept trying to take back roads. Having never driven at night, I figured that was safest. Phil and I decided we could drop the girls off at their place and just walk home from there. I was sure we'd get home at sunrise, but if we could just get the car to the girls' house I didn't care. Phil kept saying I should get on a main road and hurry it up so Sarah wouldn't puke in the car but I was too nervous. I kept looking back in the rearview to see Elizabeth looking silently miserable as she stared out the window.

We were about halfway to Sarah's house when I turned a corner and spotted a cop car slowly cruising straight toward us. Damn. Phil was right. I should have taken a main road. His headlights shined right on Phil and me as he approached and I'm sure we looked like terrified ghosts there in the dark.

"Damn, he saw us. We looked suspicious, I know it!" Phil shouted.

"Keep cool. Just keep looking forward!" I barked at him. I tried to drive normal even though I could feel my hands shaking on the wheel. I could feel the cop looking at us. Then, of course, the minute we passed him he turned on his lights.

Damn.

I could see his car swing around in the rearview mirror. I just wanted to sink down into my seat and disappear. Slowly, I pulled over to the side of the road. Sarah was freaking out in the backseat.

"My parents are going to kill me! They're gonna kill me!" she kept saying.

"Stay cool," Phil said. "All you have to tell them is that your friends were too drunk to drive and you were worried, so you drove. You kept someone from driving drunk. A cop can't get mad about that."

I hoped he was right.

"You can't tell him we're drunk! We're underage, you dumb fuck!" Sara screeched from the backseat.

"Maybe they won't ask for your license," Phil said. Just then, Sarah leaned out of her window and puked all over the side of the car. "So much for that," Phil said. He hunkered down lower in his seat.

The cop shone his flashlight into my face as he came up to the window. He looked back at the mess running down the side of the car, then at me.

"What's going on here?"

"I'm going to be completely honest with you," I told him. "We were at a party. These are some friends of mine from school. I was afraid they drank too much to drive home safely and insisted I drive them home, but here's the thing, I only have a permit. I'm eligible for my license in a couple of weeks. We're really close to their home and then I'll walk home from there."

The cop looked at me for the longest few seconds of my life. Then he looked at the girls in the back of the car. Then he leaned over to look at Phil, then back at me. He scowled under his big cop moustache.

"What's up with the haircut?" he asked in a less-than-pleasant voice. I shrugged.

"You better step out of the car," he said. In no time, I was cuffed and facing the car.

Phil was now also outside the car, cuffed. He sat on the ground next to the girls. The cop took their IDs and went back to his squad car. I stood there feeling about as helpless as I ever could have imagined feeling. I locked eyes with Phil; even in the dark it was easy to read the panic on his face. Sarah puking again in the grass where they were sitting interrupted the moment. I heard the cop's footsteps as he walked back over to me from his car.

"Driving without a license, driving a car that doesn't belong to you, no proof of insurance, underage drinking… You're in a lot of trouble. You and your freaky little friends are in a lot of trouble." He said this with great disdain. "Stay here." He walked back over to the police car.

"Psst, what did he say?" Phil asked under his breath.

I ignored him as I tried to see what the cop was doing. He was speaking on his radio. Great. He was probably calling the patty wagon or something to pick us up. I looked over to see what Elizabeth was doing. She was looking after Sarah, who was a total and absolute mess.

Another police car pulled up. A younger cop with short blonde hair and a different uniform got out. He walked over and met the moustache cop at his car. As they talked, he kept looking back over at us. I really wished I could have heard what they were saying. As I strained to listen, I thought I saw the moustache cop hand our IDs to the younger one. I returned my gaze to the ground as they started walking over in my direction.

The moustache cop spoke. "I'm with the County Sheriff's Department and you happen to be about a block out of my jurisdiction. This is Officer Reynolds from local PD. He'll be dealing with you. You're very lucky that I happened to pull you over here instead of a block back 'cause I would have come down on you hard. You got that?"

I meekly shrugged. I seemed to be doing a lot of shrugging lately.

The moustache cop pulled out his key and removed my handcuffs. He slowly swaggered back to his car. The younger cop took me by the elbow and pulled me aside.

"I want to speak with you a second."

As he walked me away from the group, I really started to worry. I once saw this English movie where these cops told a thug kid he could either take a beating right there or go to jail… Maybe this was one of those moments?

"So these guys were drunk and you thought instead of letting them drive you would drive, correct?" I was caught off guard from his tone of voice—he didn't sound as pissed as the last cop. I nodded yes.

"The smart thing to do would have been calling them a cab or getting someone else to drive them."

"I know…" I said. He looked over at Phil, who was wearing the Dead Kennedy's shirt he always wore. The shirt said, "Nazi Punks Fuck Off!" For a brief moment, I was mad at Phil for wearing that shirt. I was sure the cop was gonna give us an even harder time because of it.

"You guys into punk rock?" he asked. I nodded yes again. "Yeah, I used to listen to that stuff." He took a good look around, then raised his shirtsleeve to show me the faded black bars of a Black Flag tattoo on his arm.

"I'm going to have to write you a ticket for driving without a license. It will most likely prevent you from getting your license for a while. Sorry about that, but you should think about that the next time something like this happens."

"What about the others?" I asked.

He looked over at Sarah.

"They'll have to call someone to pick them up. They can go home. You, on the other hand—I'll have to take you back home and inform your parents of what you were doing."

Even in the dark, I could see the relief on Phil's face.

"Fair enough?" the cop asked.

"Yeah."

It was really late. I knew my parents were going to flip out when they got a knock on the door from a cop. I had to sit in the back of the car. As we drove, the cop talked about some punk shows he had been to in Oakland, California. I was too distracted to listen. All I could do was think about how busted I was gonna be. When I wasn't worrying about that, I was thinking about Elizabeth. I'd looked over at her one last time before the cop hauled me off. She hadn't even been looking my way.

When we got to my house, I listened to the cop knocking on my front door. My dad opened the door slowly. He looked at the cop, then immediately looked over at the car and me. They conversed for a moment. Then my mom appeared in the doorway. Their hushed conversation felt too much like the one between my father and the principal only too recently. The cop handed my father a pink slip of paper, they shook hands, and the cop came back over to the car. He opened the door, letting me out.

"See you around, guy."

"Thanks. Thanks for being cool about everything," I said. He nodded and got back in his car. Reluctantly, I walked toward the house.

"Are you all right?" my mom asked. I nodded yes.

My dad was already in the kitchen brewing his early morning coffee. I guess he wasn't going back to bed. He sat down in his chair and lit up his cigarette. He peered at me through the dark.

"You drove the car because you thought your friends were too drunk?"

"Yes."

"Were you drinking?"

"No." I didn't think the few sips of the warm beer earlier counted. There was a long pause as he contemplated me. I couldn't take it.

"Are you mad?" I asked.

"You were trying to do the right thing. Why would I be mad about that? You broke the law, and there will be consequences, but I'm not mad about it." He took a big drag off his cigarette. "Get some sleep."

I slept in pretty late the next day. I got up once to get some water and I overheard my mom and father talking in the other room.

"What is happening with him? All of a sudden he's getting into all this trouble and doing all of these things."

"He's just doing some *growing up*. He'll be fine."

The latter was my father's voice.

Chapter 6: The Social

When I got to school Monday, I heard from Phil how everybody else got home. Rob and Rachel actually came to pick up Sarah and Elizabeth. They took them back to their house where they spent the night. Poor Phil had to walk home alone, and he wasn't clear with me how they reached Rob and Rachel, either. Maybe they made Phil go find a payphone, and he didn't want to admit it?

The thing I couldn't believe was that when Rob picked up the girls, he told them that no cops ever actually showed up at his house. They weren't even called. That was just something his neighbor said to get rid of everybody. I got in all of that trouble and was probably going to get screwed on getting my license—and for what? For a girl who could care less about me, and another girl who was a drunken idiot? Sarah gave me the silent treatment when I saw her in the hallway and every time I saw her the rest of the day.

I asked Rob what was up with her and he didn't say much. I was beginning to think it was too easy to fall out of grace with this group. If one of them started acting weird to you, then all of a sudden the others did as well. Except for Phil. He was always cool to me no matter what, and besides, they were acting weird to him, too. To my surprise, Rachel was really nice to me at lunch.

"How awesome was that party?" She glanced at me awkwardly. "Oh, sorry about what happened," she seemed genuine. Maybe we bonded a little on those soccer fields the other night?

September had come and gone without a homecoming dance. There had been a death at the school: a jock, he was a popular senior and a member of the football team. He had gotten really drunk with some college kids and wrecked his car, killing himself. I didn't know who he was. I'd never even seen him around. But his death rippled through the school. It not only affected the school at large, but because of Toad and his big mouth, it came down on the members of the Freak Table personally…

We were all sent home early the day the news broke that the kid died. I was sitting in English class waiting for the teacher to show up. No one knew where she was and it was abnormal for her to not be there before we were. When she finally entered, it was with a somber look on her face.

"I just came from the Administrative Office. I have some unfortunate and upsetting news. Paul Gerald passed away last night."

People in the class reacted in different ways. Some girls in the corner started crying. I don't think they knew him. To most of us, death was just something that happened on TV, to people on the news, or people in "war-torn" countries or something. I didn't know how to react; I'd never really known anyone who died. My grandfather died when I was a little kid, but I hadn't been old enough to know what was going on.

The teacher dismissed class and said that for anyone who was feeling bad or wanted to show support there would be a gathering in the main gym. Everyone quietly exited into the halls and either went toward the gym or toward their lockers.

I was getting my books out of my locker when I heard Toad flying down the hallway.

"**WHOO**, out early!" he shouted. Toad wasn't the most sensitive person. I gave him a disapproving look as I slammed the door on my locker. What was he thinking? He was gonna get us killed!

"We're free, man. What do you want to do?" he asked. He hadn't noticed my dirty look or the countless people in the hallway glaring at him.

Rachel, Sarah, and Phil walked up, which luckily broke some of the tension.

"What do you guys want to go do? We don't have to go to our last class!"

Sarah spoke first. "Toad, we should go to the memorial. Be respectful."

"No way, I'm not sitting through that!"

I think he could have been cooler about it, but I also kind of agreed with him. "Let's just get out of here before people start to notice we're *not* going to the memorial."

"Well, I'm going." And with that, Sarah stormed off.

The rest of us went to a park on the way home from school and hung out. We didn't really have fun or anything... We just sat around and talked about how weird it was that somebody had died. Sitting there in that park, none of us realized the impending doom that Toad had assured for us just an hour earlier by running down the hall so excited to get out of class.

The first retaliation came the next day at school. A lot of the jock guys wouldn't mess with Toad. He was pretty intimidating. He had a reputation and they knew he could fight. So instead they went after the people smaller than him, or people who were alone. People like me or like Phil.

I was sitting at my locker eating Andy Capp's Cheddar Fries from the vending machine when Brad Thompson and his crew of letter-jacketed thugs walked over. I was quickly cornered.

"We heard what your fucking friend was saying yesterday in the halls. You pussy wavers are fucking dead!"

"What are you talking about?" I asked. I knew exactly what he was talking about. "No one's happy that poor guy got killed," I said.

I had a carton of orange juice sitting on the ground next to me. One of Brad's friends, who I recognized from science class, kicked the juice carton really hard. It exploded, splattering the lockers and me. I was soaked. Orange juice was in my eyes and dripping down my face. They didn't laugh.

"Nobody at this school likes you freaks. One of you should have died instead of someone normal!"

Brad kicked me. It hurt. It really hurt. My eyes watered up and my skin stung where his foot had made contact.

As they walked off, I fought to get my breath back. I glanced up to see that Mr. James had been watching through the glass doors of the shop rooms. As he and I made eye contact, he turned away.

I was so mad. I was mad at them for always fucking with me. I was mad at Toad for having a big mouth. I was mad at that kid Paul for getting drunk and killing himself. But I didn't want it to get worse. And I didn't feel right about Toad starting it all. So I decided not to mention what happened to anyone.

The next few weeks of school were hell. Well, every week at school was hell, but this was worse. Fights were breaking out between jocks and skaters, jocks and stoners, jocks and freaks. Toad had sparked a fire. The jocks were even talking shit to the girls like they were guys. Everyone from the Freak Table had a story about a conflict.

"Did you hear what happened to Sarah today?" Rachel asked as she sipped from her Orange Julius cup. Phil, Toad, and I had run into her at the mall. She was shopping for a dress or something and we were on our way to the skate shop.

Toad had an uncle who every now and then would send him money. There was really no explanation for it, except that he was Toad's uncle and felt bad because Toad's family never had money to buy anything.

Toad never had much, and never really wanted much. But he did need some new bearings and wheels for his board. His were starting to rust because he skated through too many puddles.

"So Sarah was in class and had to use the restroom."

"Number two or number one?" Toad asked with his devilish grin.

"Gross, Toad! Can't you act like a human being for one moment?"

"What? I need to know the details of the story."

Rachel continued while crinkling her nose at Toad. "Anyway, Sarah got up and left the classroom to use the restroom—one or two I don't know, Toad. Of course, she left all her stuff at her desk. When she got back, she found all this shit written on her textbook about being a witch and a freak. Whoever did it also stuck gum between some of the pages, too."

"That's bullshit," said Phil. I wondered if Toad had any sense that he was to blame for all of this.

"If I find out who did it, I'll kick his ass!" Toad said firmly.

"Who says it's even a guy? A lot of the preppy girls would do that, too!"

"Well, if it is a guy, I'll fuck him up."

Maybe Toad did realize what he had put us all through? But, then again, it wasn't really Toad's fault at this point. He wasn't the one making our lives hell; it was the jocks. They just needed an excuse.

"So now, at the end of semester, Sarah has to pay for the book."

"That sucks," I said.

"Yeah… It sure does—" She interrupted herself. "Oh, here's the shop I wanted to look at. You guys coming in with me?"

"Fuck no! I'm not going into a girls' clothing store!" Toad barked at her.

Phil and I laughed.

"Maybe Toad's afraid he'd find something he wanted to wear!" Rachel said with a smirk.

Phil and I cracked up.

The controversy of the home coming dance continued. We heard a lot of the jocks and their parents complaining that they wanted to see a game and a dance go on like normal, that the game should be in Paul's honor and all that. "A tribute to the boy"… I don't think the school wanted to advertise that one of their football heroes died while driving drunk. So the administration canceled homecoming.

What they did decide to do was have a dance at the end of October for Halloween. They were calling it the Halloween Social.

All the members of the Freak Table rejoiced at the idea of having a Halloween event. It was like a holiday and party just for us. Unfortunately, it turned into yet another clash between the normal kids and the kids like us.

I was too busy with other things to really care about the social. I had been busy doing work for my dad in an effort to raise money for my own skateboard. There were a couple of Powell Peralta decks I had been eyeballing and some G&S trucks I wanted. All of my free time was dedicated to raising that money.

Phil had recorded a New Order concert off the college radio station in Fort Collins one night and made me a copy. It was awesome. I didn't have the money to spare on music, so I was happy he'd given me the tape. It was some radio show for something called Westwood One *Modern Rock Live*. I must have listened to that tape over a hundred times in just one month. I would listen to it on my Walkman everywhere I went, every time I was doing yard work, or any time I was sitting at home. I just kept listening to it over and over. I didn't even know the names of the songs, but it didn't matter. I had them memorized by heart. I even had some of the shouts from people in the crowd memorized.

Before we knew it, the Halloween Social had arrived. I didn't dress up at school. I was already embarrassed most of the time at school anyway. I didn't want to give anyone further fuel to use against me. Phil had a postal worker costume. His uncle was a mailman, so every year he used his uncle's extra clothes. This year the twist was that he was "going postal."

Rob dressed up. He wore some sheets as if they were a toga. You could tell he was going to get out of high school and fit in nicely at a college somewhere—where he was bound to be drunk and wearing a toga often. Rachel also dressed up. It seemed the two of them were good at having fun. Her costume was this tight Cleopatra-type deal and insanely sexy. I couldn't believe none of us had realized what an amazing body she had. She was getting attention from every guy in school, even the normal ones. Girls noticed, too. Some of the preppy girls seemed a little jealous. I don't think Rachel planned for it, but people looked at her differently from that day.

Toad had a poor choice for a Halloween costume and Phil and I had to make him take it off before we went to school. We were standing in his driveway waiting for him when he came out of his house in some old letter jacket and all covered in fake blood.

"I'm a dead jock, guys."

Unbelievable. I looked over at Phil, and judging from the look on his face he couldn't believe it, either.

"Are you trying to get us fucking killed, Toad?"

"Dude, you have to go change right now!"

"If you wear that, we're fucking dead. I can't even walk around with you anymore if you wear that!"

"All right, you pussies," he said. "I'll just be a skater who got hit by a car."

With those words he reluctantly went back inside to change.

When we got to school, we found that a group of lame jock guys, including Brad Thompson, were wearing as much black clothes as they could find, and make-up. They were walking around telling people they were "wavers." I didn't think they were funny.

"See, I should have worn the fucking letter jacket!" Toad said.

Maybe he was right?

Luckily, we didn't have to dress for gym if we didn't want to. Afterward, on my way to English, I had a strange interaction with Sarah in the hallway. She grabbed me when no one else was around.

"Why didn't you dress up?" she asked.

I shrugged. "I didn't feel like it, I guess."

What did she care about my Halloween costume? She hadn't said a word to me since the night of the party.

"I'm sorry about the past couple of weeks. I was so drunk that night I blacked out. I just remembered pieces of it and didn't realize you were trying to help out until Phil and Elizabeth filled me in on the details. I'm also really sorry about you getting the ticket and everything."

I was annoyed it had taken her so long to talk to me about it. I guess I didn't care, though. I was happy that she and I were getting along again, and even more happy that it sounded like Elizabeth might have said something to defend me.

Because it was Halloween, our art teacher brought in a video for us to watch instead of doing work. It was on Ansel Adams and it was pretty boring. I sat there trying to steal glances of Elizabeth. The way she looked under the flashing light of the TV screen reminded me of how she'd looked that night on the soccer fields. Her body raised and lowered softly as she breathed. And then class was over.

After school, Toad and I were walking through the parking lot when were confronted by Brad and his goons.

"Can we hang out with you guys, now?" Brad asked from behind his poor make-up job. "We want to be wavers like you."

"I'm punk rock, motherfucker! You got a problem with that?" Toad shouted. Gotta love Toad sometimes. I didn't think the jock guys were expecting us to say anything back to them because they had us so outnumbered. They were at a loss for words. Luckily, Rob and Rachel pulled up in their car.

"You guys looking for a ride?" Rob asked. His timing couldn't have been better. I shot a dirty look at Brad and his friends as I got into the car.

"Hey, Rachel, too bad you hang out with the freaks 'cause you're looking hot today, momma!" Brad said.

As his friends laughed, Rob leaned out of the window of his car. With a friendly voice and a smile on his face he said, "That's my *sister,* man. Be careful what you say!"

And that was that. Brad shut his mouth. Rob was one of those people who fit in with everyone. I don't think someone who wanted to remain popular would cross him.

"Maybe we'll see you at the dance tonight, Rachel," Brad said as we drove away.

Toad almost leaped out of the moving car to go after him.

"Don't let 'em get to you," Rob coolly told Toad. "They've got nothing on us." Although Toad kind of had a big mouth, I really envied that he stood up for himself so unhesitatingly. He wouldn't take shit from anyone and I liked that about him. I wished I was a little more like that myself. But I wasn't. I always let people get away with too much.

"Are you going to the dance tonight?" Rachel asked as we pulled up to my house.

"Probably not."

"I think Elizabeth is going with us…"

I know she thought that would get me there. And she was right. All of a sudden the idea of going was at least an option. They said bye and drove away.

A couple hours later, I had finally convinced Phil to go to the dance.

"Listen. I really want to go and see Elizabeth. I never get to be around her except for fucking art class, and you know how that is! Besides, Sarah will be there and I know you won't mind seeing her, either."

He mulled it over and reluctantly agreed. We then discussed the effects of Rachel's Halloween costume on our amateur libidos.

Phil continued wearing his postal outfit. He tried to get me to dress up but I still didn't want to. I did break down and borrowed some of my mom's eyeliner before we left for the dance.

"Are you going as Phil's date?" my dad asked, looking at the thick black around my eyes.

"No way!" I said.

My father looked at me wearily.

"Maybe you should use a mirror next time," he said.

Phil cracked up laughing. My mom laughed, too. I'm glad my dad was making jokes, though, because I could tell he really didn't like me wearing it.

"Do you boys need a ride?" my mother asked. I told her we were fine and didn't want to be seen getting dropped off.

"Be careful and stay out of trouble."

I nodded and shrugged as always.

"Phil, you don't let him drive anyone else's car if you can help it."

Phil started cracking up again.

The neighborhood was alive with small packs of trick-or-treaters making the rounds in costume. As we walked toward the school, Phil would join packs of kids walking up to houses asking for candy. He was mostly snubbed but a couple of confused people actually gave him some.

When we got to the school and into the gym, the main lights had been turned out. There was a DJ in the corner with a small set-up of pathetic disco lights and a cheap-looking disco ball on a table. As I was trying to find someone I knew, a woman dressed as a witch walked over to me. It was my teacher from Great Leaders.

"Nice to see you," she said. "How are you getting along in your new classes?"

I told her how things were going. I also told her that I still had to deal with jerks in other classes but that it wasn't as bad. Then luckily, Phil spotted some of the others.

I said bye to the teacher quickly as Phil and I walked over to meet everyone. They were in the corner over by the DJ, hanging out.

Sarah greeted us. "Hey, you guys. The DJ's really cool. He's excited that we're here and he's been playing all kinds of good stuff. He even played The Smiths!" She gave us both hugs. I noticed that Toad wasn't there among them. I didn't think he'd show up but was kind of hoping, just in case a fight broke out. Rob and Rachel had changed out of their costumes. I think Rachel might have been tired of all the extra attention.

Phil and I were slumped against the wall waiting for better music to come on when Elizabeth came in. She was dressed in what looked like a gown from Cinderella or some Shakespearean play. She was unbelievably beautiful. The lights from the disco ball slowed down around her as she walked through the crowd. Rachel and Sarah greeted her with even more squeals and hugs than normal. Rob flattered her, telling her how pretty she looked, and I just sat there staring blankly. Phil nudged me in the side.

"Dude, she looks hot!" he said.

Instead of continuing to gawk, I tried to play it cool and act like I didn't notice she had arrived. I don't know why I did that—it just seemed like the best thing to do at the time.

Phil and I went to go get something to drink. The concession stand they usually used for basketball games was open. We purchased soda that was in soggy paper cups, flat, and lacking of ice. When we got back to the group, Sarah snuck some rum into Phil's drink for him. I was uncomfortable drinking, so I opted not to. I envied her ingenuity, though. She had filled a couple of pill bottles with rum from Rachel's house. They were airtight and small enough to sneak in several of them.

As we were hanging out, Phil leaned into me with a grin. "I'm feeling all warm from that shot of rum," he said.

Elizabeth leaned against the wall, talking with Rachel. In her costume, she looked like she was waiting for a knight in shining armor to come to her aid and whisk her off into the sunset. Instead she had me, standing there goofy, clutching a flat soda, and looking as insecure as someone could.

The DJ played a slow song and I did something very, very stupid. Some guy I didn't know came over and started slow dancing with Rachel. Much to his excitement, Phil got to dance with Sarah. As they walked out onto the dance floor, he flashed a thumbs-up at me. I wasn't sure where Rob and the others were, but as luck had it Elizabeth and I were the only ones left hanging out by the wall. I really wanted to ask her to dance. But logic told me not to. She never talked to me. She never even looked at me that much. She wasn't interested. I wanted to ask her, I wanted her to say yes, and I wanted to be out there with my arms around her.

Rachel broke away from her friend and came over to me.

"You should ask her to dance," she insisted. "She's all alone over there and I know you want to." I shouldn't have, but my longing, in combination with Rachel's encouragement, set me into motion.

"Elizabeth," I said. It was the first time I had ever said her name directly to her. It felt strange. She turned and looked down at me, her shoes giving her extra height. That didn't help my confidence. She smiled politely.

"Do you wanna dance?" I asked.

An eternity passed while I waited for her reply. She smiled uncomfortably and spoke.

"You seem really nice but I'm just not… I really don't feel like dancing."

Something inside of me turned black and ugly. Something sticky and evil, like in a horror movie. I didn't know if I should stand there and try to make conversation or just walk away. All I knew was that suddenly I felt like a fool. Like everyone in the gymnasium was looking over at us, and that I was some kind of village idiot.

Flat soda. Thank god for flat soda! I realized that was my way out.

"I'm going to go get something else to drink, did you want anything?"

That seemed like the safest way to crawl away with my tail between my legs.

"No thanks," she said with an awkward smile.

I walked off, bumping into a couple of people trying to get away as fast as possible.

I got over to the concession stand and ordered another sorry-ass coke. I sat there contemplating my flat soda and feeling like someone had just socked me in the stomach. I'm sure there was internal bleeding. I hid by the concession stand for as long as I could. After a few songs had passed, I reluctantly walked back to the others.

"Here's a set for my crew over here in the corner," the DJ said over his crappy PA. I really wished he wouldn't have done that. It was going to draw attention to us and that was the last thing we needed. I had heard the song he was playing once before. "Nothing Compares to You" by Sinead O'Conner. It was a slow song and a sad one. Once again, everyone started slow dancing. Well, everyone in our corner. Everyone else was busy gawking at us. Phil went back over to dance with Sarah. Rob was back from wherever he had gone and was now slow dancing with Elizabeth. It stung like salt in a wound when I looked over and saw it.

How could he do that to me? What a fucking jerk! Then Rachel came over and sat down next to me. She saw the look on my face.

"Don't worry about it," she said. "We've all known each other forever. It doesn't mean anything."

"Yeah, I know. It's not him. It's her. She told me she didn't feel like dancing."

Rachel shrugged. We sat there and watched as the song went on. It was the first time I realized that Elizabeth was the girl I was never going to get. Some of the other kids from school went back to what they were doing. Others actually started dancing. And some, of course, were standing around making fun of us.

I was so focused on feeling sorry for myself that I didn't notice who had walked up until it was too late. Brad Thompson. He was standing there in front of Rachel and me. What the hell did he want now? Then he leaned over. Not to me, but to Rachel.

"Do you want to go dance?" he asked her. I couldn't believe what I was hearing. That fucker. He and his jock friends who were too good for any of us, who ridiculed everything we did, had now realized Rachel was a sexy girl and now he wanted to dance with her. I just couldn't believe it. I looked over at her for her response.

"No thanks, I don't feel like dancing right now," she said.

Good girl! She shot me a look out of the corner of her eye.

"Figures, you freaks!" he said as he stormed away.

"Fuck him," I said. "He doesn't know you're too good for him." She smiled and agreed. She talked for the rest of the song about how much she hated going to school with these people. Brad had been an interruption, but in the back of my mind I was still thinking about how Elizabeth had shot me down. The song ended and then with a small crash, I heard the beginning of something that amazed me.

The DJ put on a song I had never heard before. Rachel sprang up with an excited squeal and grabbed my hand, pulling me onto the dance floor with her. It seemed by the time we got out there, everybody else was already dancing.

"What song is this?"

Rachel looked at me like I was crazy. "'Just Like Heaven'—The Cure." And that was that. As the lights moved around the gym, I half closed my eyes and listened to every piece of the song. Every beat. Every time the chorus came through. We danced and carried on. I was moved inside. All that mattered to me was that moment, that song, and my friends.

Maybe I should have noticed everything else that was going on...for instance, the fact that, except for our little group, the entire school had stopped dancing. Led by a few key people like Brad, they had surrounded all of us in our corner.

The jock bastards took turns darting in and out of our small group and making fun of us. I got bumped hard a couple of times. We all tried to keep dancing and ignoring them. The only time I stopped dancing was when some jerk bumped Sarah too hard and Phil got between the guy and her.

"Watch it!" Phil shouted over the music. I had never seen Phil look pissed before.

I moved over to back him up.

Fuckers. They weren't going to ruin it for me. They weren't going to ruin it for us. We kept trying to enjoy ourselves until the song ended. Then, instinctually, we made our way back to the wall. The mob dispersed and that was the end of any good music being played for the night. I think the DJ wanted to keep us from getting lynched.

After the incident, most of the members of our group left the dance. Phil and I had to wait for our ride, so we went outside and kept a low profile by The Slab. Rob had offered a ride, but I didn't feel like riding with him after seeing him and Elizabeth dancing together. I opted to wait for my dad, and Phil, being a good friend, said he'd stay with me. One by one, the others disappeared. I wasn't sure when Elizabeth, Sarah, and Rachel had left.

My father picked us up. He took us by an all night drive-through and we ate in the car while he reminisced about some of his high school dances.

"Don't you dare repeat any of this to your mother," he cautioned us, "and while we're at it, you better not tell her I was eating this junk after ten o'clock, either!"

Phil and I chuckled.

Later, after we dropped off Phil, I was back home sitting in my bedroom. I listened to my tape of New Order from the radio. I couldn't sleep, so I looked out the window with some binoculars that belonged to my father.

As the music played, I peered through the lenses at the cars that passed every so often. I looked at the dark silhouettes in each car, wondering who they were and where they were going to, or coming from. I also thought about how earlier in the night Elizabeth had rejected me again, and about all the jocks who kept screwing with us. I didn't remember falling asleep.

Chapter 7: Half-pipe

W hen I got up the next day, I headed straight to the mall and went to the music store. My mission for the weekend was to find that song "Just Like Heaven." I looked through all of the tapes and couldn't find the right album. I didn't know what to do. It was the only record store within walking distance and they didn't have what I wanted.

They had other Cure albums, but not the one with the song that I was sure I could not live without. I looked through the art on the other albums and decided to pick up *Killing an Arab*. It looked good. And it had a song called "10:15 Saturday Night" on it. The name of that song reminded me of the night before when I'd been watching out my window, so that was the album I bought.

I made a stop by the skate shop, which was now a weekend pilgrimage for me. They didn't seem to have too much that was new and I was starting to get tired of torturing myself looking at boards I couldn't afford.

Walking home, I ran into this guy Steve. I'd noticed him before. It was hard not to with his tall hair and knee-high boots. Steve was older than me. I figured he was probably out of high school. He always had on a black trench coat and wore his brown hair up in double fins. His boots had huge metal shin plates on them, so they looked like something out of *Road Warrior*. Though I had seen Steve walking up and down the street for years, I'd never talked to him. He never had any reason to talk to me, either. But I guess now that I was looking more like a skater all the time, he finally decided to talk to me when I passed him.

He took off his earphones and said something. I couldn't hear him because of my own, so I pulled them off my ears.

"How's it going, man?" he asked.

"Not bad. It's Saturday, right? I don't have to be at school." I didn't know what else to say. This guy always looked so cool; I was intimidated.

"You coming from the mall?"

I nodded.

"What are you listening to?"

I pulled out the tape and showed him.

"Cool. Getting into The Cure, huh?"

Steve looked like he had been everywhere and done everything so I was a little embarrassed to admit that I was just buying my first Cure album.

"Yeah, just trying to complete my collection," I told him. "Don't have this one yet." He smiled and nodded like he knew what I meant.

"What are you listening to?" I asked.

"Skinny Puppy. You should check 'em out, man. Really good music, means something, ya know?"

"I'll have to check them out one of these days," I said. He started rummaging around in his pockets. Then he then removed his Walkman and ejected the tape. He handed it to me.

"Here, man, just take this. It's a copy of a record I have at home." I reluctantly reached out; after all, I didn't have anything to offer him in return.

"Thanks, thanks, but I don't really have anything to trade you or anything," I told him.

"Don't worry about it. You really need to know about Skinny Puppy. They're fucking great. Besides, I like the idea of someone else in this shitty hick town listening to some real music."

We shook hands.

"Thanks!"

"See you around."

"Yeah, see you around."

He continued on his way and I continued on mine. How cool was that guy? The whole way home I marveled about the silent understanding that we had between us.

It was good that the weekend was relaxing because school was horrible the next week. I was suffering through my English teacher lecture on how one day we'd come to appreciate Beowulf when I overheard this guy Tom. He was one of the jock bastards who'd been with Brad the day my skateboard went into the gutter. I couldn't hear everything he was saying, but it had to do with Rachel and Brad at the dance and it didn't sound good. In hushed voices they were dropping words like "blowjob" and "bushes."

"What did you just say?" I said in an abrasive voice. I spoke without even realizing I was going to speak. The entire class fell silent. I must have interrupted the teacher.

"As I was saying, in the story, he is a hero. But by today's standards—" I interrupted again, turning back to Tom.

"What did you just say?" I asked Tom.

"Mind your own business, *waver*," Tom barked back at me. The teacher interrupted us both, asking for quiet until the end of class. I spent the rest of the lecture hearing their hushed, snickering voices. I didn't know what was going on, but I didn't like the idea of these guys talking about one of *my* friends.

On the way home, I told Phil what happened and he didn't think too much of it. We met up with Toad, and he and Phil skated. I just hung around and talked with them. Since I wasn't moving around like them, I was freezing my ass off.

"If you're cold, why don't you dance around and entertain us? That'll warm you up," Toad said.

"You can be our cheerleader!" Phil blurted out. They cracked up. I didn't think it was that funny.

By lunch the next day, there were rumors floating around the many different social groups of the school about how Rachel had given Brad a BJ at the dance. The details of the story varied depending on who was telling it.

A couple of preppy girls were talking about how Brad gave Rachel a ride home from the dance and they had this magical romantic moment in his car and knew that even though they were from different social circles they knew they had to be together.

A different group of girls who happened to be cheerleaders were overheard going on about how this waver slut tried to get Brad to go with her and how he rejected her because she was a freak.

Then you had the version from this stoner guy Lenny. He had "heard" that this freaky chick and a jock broke into the principal's office and boned right on his desk. And then, when they were finished, they tried to steal their student reports.

It was during this version of the story that Phil and I headed back in from The Slab and tried to find out what was going on. We got to the Freak Table to find Rachel and the rest of the girls absent. No Sarah, no Elizabeth, no Rachel, and also no Rob. When I got to art class, Elizabeth was there. After a few awkward moments of pretending not to notice her and do my work I turned to her.

"Elizabeth, about the dance last Friday?" I said. A nervous look shot across her face. Her eyes went from me to Chad and his friend behind us and then back to me. "Is everything okay with Rachel?"

"Whatever is going on with Rachel is her business," Elizabeth quipped back in a measured tone. "She has the right to privacy and to not have people talking about her."

Wow. Elizabeth had just snapped at me. She snapped at *me*! I didn't know what to say. I retreated back into working on my latest project, a poor attempt at a Georgia O'Keefe-type cow skull. I swished around the paint for a while, focusing more on how insulted I felt than on the work I was supposed to be doing. Toward the end of class, she got up and left the room. When she was gone, I felt a nudge on my back. Surprised and wary, I turned around to see what *they* wanted. Chad talked in an informative but quiet voice.

"Hey, dude. Yesterday at practice, Brad was bragging about how Elizabeth's friend Rachel ended the night of the dance by giving him one hell of a hummer." He didn't sound like he was trying to be a jerk, which confused me. He shrugged and went back to doing his work.

My blood was starting to boil. That fucker Brad had gone up to her at the dance. She had refused him and now he was going around the school telling everyone this? Even his friends were! It's no wonder Rachel and her friends were nowhere to be found.

When I did see Rachel the next day, she was silent except at lunch when some girls walked by snickering and she rushed off toward the bathroom with tears in her eyes. Sarah ran after her. Phil and I just sat there at the table feeling useless. We were so pissed and there was nothing we could do.

"If I catch him saying anything, I'm gonna beat his ass!" Phil said.

"Yeah, I wanna knock that guy's teeth out," I agreed.

The two of us sounded pretty tough, whispering to each other in the lunchroom.

Rob interrupted us with, "Guys, just mind your own business. Don't go picking a fight and making it worse. Things will work themselves out."

Rob was always so mellow. I never saw him get mad. In some ways I couldn't stand it. Yes, everyone liked him. Yes, he never seemed to generate friction or be the target of it, but something about that frustrated me. The way I figured, if someone was doing something to make you mad, or trying to take advantage of you, then you had the right to get pissed and do something about it. Not that I ever did.

Phil and I ended the lunch period looking at the empty doorway to the girls' restroom, wondering what was going on inside and why they wouldn't let us do anything to help.

Although still troubled by what was going on with Rachel—the rumors and all the damn jocks—I tried to be in a good mood the following day because it was my birthday. At lunch, Rob, Rachel, Sarah, and Phil snuck off to a nearby convenience store and bought a cupcake and a candle. We all got yelled at for having an open flame in the cafeteria when they lit the candle and brought it over to me. Nevertheless, I was glad that everything seemed a little more back to normal.

Toad didn't know it was my birthday but swore up and down he would get me something good later. He was always swearing something like that and you always knew it wouldn't happen. Not that it mattered. In his own way, Toad was a good guy and I knew he never even had the money for the things he needed.

Elizabeth leaned over toward the end of art class.

"Sarah told me it was your birthday today. Happy birthday!"

That was the best birthday present I could have asked for. She didn't say anything else. And after she said it she slipped right back into her look of concentration, focused on her assignment. I must have been beaming.

Phil and I walked home after school without Toad. We'd seen him going out to The Slab with some gangster kids so we figured he was probably smoking a joint.

After my dad got home from work, we picked up Phil and went to a Furs Cafeteria. My parents had given me the choice of going somewhere really nice just the three of us, or going somewhere kind of normal and bringing Phil along. I knew my dad loved going to these cafeterias so it seemed like a good idea.

There was an awkward moment when my mom had asked why she never saw Wes around anymore.

"Now that he's on the basketball team he acts like a jerk."

"Yeah, that guy sold out!" Phil blurted out.

I think my father was amused with Phil's choice of words.

"Sold out, huh?"

"Yeah, he totally turned his back on the skater lifestyle, you know? Just so he could fit in with the majority."

"People do that sometimes," my father said.

I continued stirring my mashed potatoes with my fork. I didn't know what my father thought of me hanging around with kids who used terms like "the majority" and "sold out."

When we got home, we broke out the small cake my mom had made. It was pretty good and she'd tried to decorate it with a frosting skateboard, which was kind of dorky. But I appreciated it anyway.

After the cake, my mom excitedly entered the room with an unwrapped box containing a Steve Caballero deck. It had G&S trucks and black Slimeballs wheels.

"How did you know how to get all this?" I asked in shock.

They had pieced together everything I wanted. It was an awesome board!

"We had some help from Phil," my father said.

Phil came over and shook my hand. "Happy birthday, man!"

He handed me a small package the size of a cassette. "Here, this is from me."

I opened it to find the Cure album I had been looking for, the one with "Just Like Heaven" on it. I told them all thanks time and time again. I was in shock. What an awesome birthday!

"There's something else," my mother said, smiling. My father's face was as serious as always, but I could tell he was trying to not crack a smile. The man was always trying to keep his cool.

"It's going to take some time and you'll have to be patient because he's never built anything like this before, but your father came across a large amount of spare lumber on one of his last jobs."

The suspense was killing me. What were they talking about? What were they going to build? It wasn't making any sense. I looked over at Phil and he looked like he was about to burst.

"You're father's going to build you a half-pipe in the backyard. He's checked everything out and we should have enough room and it shouldn't be a problem with the neighbors."

I couldn't believe it. I just couldn't believe it. How could I possibly thank them for this? I looked over at Phil again, who was grinning from ear to ear.

"You knew about this?" I asked him.

"It was killing me! It was killing me not to blab about it!" he said, cracking up.

"I told him I was going to come after him with the staple gun if he said anything to you," my father joked.

So that was that. I had a new board and the promise of a half-pipe on the way. I was beaming. My own half-pipe in the backyard—that was every skater's dream. Even the dream of mediocre skaters like myself. Who knew, maybe after logging enough hours in the backyard, up and down the pipe, I'd be good enough to go pro? At the very least, the guys I skated with would finally take me more seriously… A half-pipe. Visions of grandeur began leaking into my head.

There were not a lot of swimming pools in Colorado, which meant no empty pools to skate in the winter or anything. And there were probably even fewer half-pipes. There were always rumors and legends of a half-pipe in this neighborhood or that town, but to have one of my own… To be part of the local legend… I was stunned. Every skater would be welcome there—it would be a refuge!

The next day was Friday. All I had to do was get through one crappy day of school and the weekend would be there. Phil and I were going to skate after school. I could finally skate again instead of just watching the other guys. I finally had my own board. It wasn't handed-down; every scratch on it would belong to me. It had an awesome nose, wheels that kicked ass, and even the grip tape was cool. They had put a new clear grip tape on it so you could see the graphics underneath. All I had to do to enjoy it was endure one more day of school. Easier said than done.

School was pure hell that day. For some reason, the gym teacher was riding Phil and me harder than usual, so we had to run laps the entire class while the teacher came outside to make sure we did. It was like one of those prison or WWII movies where if you fell down or stopped running you got shot or something.

Then, at lunch, we found out that some girls in one of Rachel's classes were teasing her about the whole Brad rumor.

Rob was off campus somewhere getting lunch. So it was just Phil, Toad, Sarah, and me listening to Rachel.

"I was sitting in class and I kept hearing snickering going on behind me. Well, more snickering than usual. Every time I turned around, these girls would choke back laughter like I didn't know what was going on. It kept going. I really wish I had one of you guys in that class because I was totally alone, so they could just keep fucking with me. Anyway, I finally turned around and found this guy Jay, who is an asshole, pushing a banana in and out of his mouth and pointing at me."

She broke off for a moment. The Freak Table was silent. Then in a saddened tone, she murmured, "I'm so sick of this school."

She was past the stage of crying. Now she was just depressed. It really pissed me off. I could tell Toad and Phil were pissed as well.

"I'm gonna go kick his ass right now," Toad said as he got up. "Anybody know what class this guy's in?" Everyone at the table shook their heads no.

Sarah spoke up. "Hey, didn't they say if you got in one more fight you were going to get kicked out?"

Toad nodded yes. "I don't give a fuck," he said under his breath.

Once again, I envied his total disregard for consequences. Rachel asked him to just sit back down. Just then, a carton of milk flew out of nowhere to erupt in a white explosion in the middle of our table. Milk splashed everywhere. People in the cafeteria screamed and hollered.

"You pricks!" Toad said, while flipping off as many people as he could. He was scanning the entire room with a glare, each hand raised, middle fingers up. "I'll find out who did it!"

As Toad continued his defiance toward the entire lunchroom, the girls rushed off to the bathroom to clean off the milk. I heard one of them talking about how nasty it would be if it dried and went sour. Phil just sat there. Usually these things didn't seem to bother him as much as they did me, but this time Phil looked pissed.

"Can't we have one fucking lunch without something happening?" he asked.

He was right. Not a day went by that there wasn't some drama going on for one of us. Was that what growing up was supposed to be like? One of the teachers walking by assumed that we made the mess. She made Phil, Toad, and I clean it up.

I didn't think I was going to make it through the day, I didn't think any of us would. But after lunch, some good news came through. The reason Rob wasn't around was because he'd been off making flyers for another party. He talked his parents into getting a cabin in Breckenridge up in the mountains for the weekend. Rob's plan was to surprise Rachel by throwing another party. I think it was his way of cheering her up after everything that had gone on.

The flyer read, "Sweater Party at Robbie and Rachel's. It's getting cold, so if you want free booze, wear your fucking sweater!" The word "fucking" was cleverly blacked out so you could still read it. I don't think that Rob understood Rachel's definition of "Sweater Party" when he made the flyer but the sentiment was there nonetheless.

There was a quiet buzz by the end of the day. All of the party people, the stoners, the freaks—they all had something to look forward to. Rob and Rachel's last party had been so great…until it got broken up and I got pulled over by the cops. But besides that, it had been great and I was ready for another. I agreed with Phil to get drunk myself this time so I wouldn't be tempted to be anyone's designated driver. Not the best logic, I guess…

Phil and I headed home to grab my board. We met up with Toad and skated for hours. Toad was a really good skater, maybe it was because he was so fearless. He could pull off tricks fast, and he was never afraid to try crazy things that Phil and I would never attempt. When Toad hit the ground, he'd just pop right back up laughing. Usually the worse the wipeout, the funnier he thought it was. Because of his lack of common sense, he really pulled off some cool tricks.

We were skating this drainage ditch that had this curve to it. It was kind of like a weak half-pipe, which prompted us to tell Toad about the half-pipe my dad was going to build.

"Dude, what's a poser like you gonna do with a half-pipe in your backyard? You're gonna break your fucking neck!"

He was kind of right about that. I had no idea how to skate a pipe, but I could learn. And that wasn't what was important. He should have been happy about it for me, and not only for me but for all of us because we were all going to use it.

Toad chilled out after I assured him it would be there for all of us whenever we wanted to skate it. I knew my parents would be cool about it. I imagined a happier world where once the half-pipe was finished any skater in the neighborhood would be welcomed and could skate without getting hassled. By the time Phil and I were finished telling Toad what it would be like, he was getting just as excited about it as we were.

Toad then changed the subject by making fun of me because I didn't want to rail slide on anything.

"I don't want to rub all of the graphics off the bottom of my board! I just got it," I said, defending myself.

"What good is having it if you're not going to skate it?" he asked. Maybe it was that philosophy that kept everything in Toad's house looking so worn-out.

We set course for the grocery store. It was nice being able to get where we wanted quickly now that I had a board again. I was crouching down and swerving back and forth because we were moving fast downhill. It was great until I heard the dreaded battle cry shouted from a car passing by.

"PUSSY SKATERS!"

"FUCK YOU!" Toad screamed at the top of his lungs. We saw break lights. The car swerved sharply into the turn lane ahead, cutting us off. Phil was way ahead, so the car was between him and us. It was dark but I thought I saw Phil take off running in the distance.

A bunch of older jock guys jumped out of the car. Everything went down quickly—a mess of bodies in the dark. One guy took off in Phil's direction as two others moved toward Toad. Two more were running toward me.

I swerved left, hitting grass, flying off my board and into the field next to the sidewalk. I heard my board clank and bounce away behind me as I ate dirt. Rocks dug into my back as I rolled. I jumped to my feet as fast as I could to prepare for the coming attack.

The first thing I noticed when I looked up, to my horror, was that one of the bastards had split off to pick up my board. I dodged the guy coming after me and ran toward my board as fast as I could. He beat me to it and with a twist like an Olympian he tossed my board way off into the darkness. He was rabid with delight.

"Fucking skater!"

Over his shoulder I could see Toad taking on three of the guys and losing. I started running toward them. The guy who had just tossed my board tried to block my path but I got past him with a shove. I got to Toad, right as he hit one of the guys in the face with his board. It made a loud SMACK. The guy grabbed his face, stumbling backward. Soon they were scurrying off to their car while laughing and screaming. The one was still holding his face in pain.

In the distance, Phil was just passing under a streetlight near the grocery store. With a squeal, the car peeled out. They honked their horn as they sped in his direction.

"We gotta help Phil!" I shouted at Toad.

I found my board in the dark, grabbed it, and we were off. I've never skated faster in my life. I was kicking as hard as I possibly could. Toad was doing the same. He looked ferocious. It didn't look like he had been hurt in the fight, and he was just as determined to get to Phil as I was.

As we got closer we saw the car pass under the same streetlights Phil had just passed under. We cut through the corner of the field. By the time we got into the grocery store parking lot, the jock guys were climbing back into their car.

One of them flipped us off and shouted, "Next time you better watch your mouth, pussy skaters!"

I looked around. Where was Phil? No evidence of him. I was worried. Where the hell was he? I looked around the parking lot for a slumped body or something. We rushed inside the grocery store to try to find him. The clerk looked at us like we were crazy.

Toad rushed back outside the store to look around. I followed him. Now we were desperate. Did they fucking grab Phil or kick his ass so bad he couldn't call for help?

"Psst, you guys. I'm up here. I'm up here!" We hadn't thought about looking up. Who would have? We raised our heads to find Phil grinning down at us from the roof of the grocery store. He had somehow managed to ditch his board and climb a ladder that went up to the roof. After he explained everything, we went around back, grabbed his board, and found the metal ladder he was talking about. Making sure no one saw us, we scaled the ladder, too.

Phil was stooped down low, keeping a lookout for the car of jocks. He adjusted his cap as he turned toward us.

"That was close, man."

"We thought you were dead."

"Yeah, we thought you were a goner."

"What happened to you guys?"

"He ate shit on his board so they all came after me!"

"That had to be the same car that came after me that one day!"

"Those fuckers!"

"Yeah."

"They looked old enough to be in college."

"Yeah, what are they doing chasing us?"

"That was fucking great, man! We got away!"

"I thought they got ol' Phil, man, I thought they killed you! And you're up here fucking taking it easy…"

We hung out on the roof for a while. It was really cool to be up there away from everything. It was the kind of roof that for some reason had been covered with gravel. The edges of the walls rose up, making it a very good hiding place. There was no way anyone could see us up there, so we were safe. We agreed it was our new hiding place in case we were ever outnumbered again while skating.

Phil kept insisting that the car that chased us was the same one that had come after him the day he rented *The Search for Animal Chin*. Toad and I gazed off into the distance at the sea of amber streetlights. All these tiny little specks of orange light laid flat across the black of the neighborhoods. The night air was still and brisk. Silence surrounded us.

I found the orange soda rocket Wes had shot up there. It was pretty sun-bleached. I laughed.

As we sat up there, our conversation went from our temporary pride in our escape to being fed up with always being under attack. We were excited we'd gotten away, but weren't necessarily proud of always having to run. Conversation turned to the previous week at school and everything that had happened to Rachel and how pissed off we were.

"Why don't we get some payback on one of these jock bastards for fucking with us?" Toad said.

Phil and I were all ears.

"We're sitting on top of a grocery store. Everything we need is just waiting below. Toilet paper, shaving cream, toothpaste, eggs."

A smile grew on Phil's face.

"The only problem is that I've only got like five bucks, man."

Phil, on the other hand, was pro on the teepee agenda and had the money to finance it.

Twenty bucks, thirty-six rolls of toilet paper, two cans of shaving cream, a tube of toothpaste, and a carton of eggs later and we were on our way. We made a stop by my place to ditch our boards and a stop by Toad's place to grab his familiar large duffle bag.

We then started the long walk toward our target.

"So where are we headed again?"

"That guy Tom lives in my neighborhood. We're getting him!" Phil assured us.

We took residential streets that had no traffic. Every time we saw headlights we ducked down into someone's yard or bushes to avoid being seen. It was late enough that if anyone saw us they'd know we were up to no good.

Phil and I continued ducking every time cars came by but Toad got tired of it and told us we were acting like pussies. Of course, the one time he didn't rush and hide in the bushes or someone's yard it was a cop car that was driving by.

Phil and I were hidden deep down in some really uncomfortable pine bushes as we watched anxiously. The cop car slowed down as it passed Toad but then kept going. He was carrying the duffle bag and he really looked out of place there in the neighborhood...but the car kept going.

"I can't believe it!"

"I can't believe he didn't stop!"

"Holy shit, that was close!"

"Toad, you have to hide with us next time!"

"What? They probably thought I was some punk kid who got kicked out of his house or something. Maybe I'm on my way to the train station to hitch a ride to Chicago or New York."

Toad's story about the punk's journey away from his broken home continued until Phil spotted something.

"HEADLIGHTS!" They were almost already shining on us. The cop must have gone back around the block or turned or something. Phil took off running into some nearby bushes. I had nowhere to hide except under a truck that was parked in a driveway. We yelled at Toad to just keep walking and acting normal.

We were fucked. The last thing I needed was to get in trouble with the cops again.

The headlights drew closer. To my shock, they didn't stop at Toad. They kept going and drove right up into the driveway to where I was. It must have been the people who lived at the house. And there I was hiding under their truck! The headlights illuminated the entire area underneath the truck, reflecting off some spots of oil. I was trying to stay behind one of the wheels. How could they not see me? How were they not jumping out of the car and trying to kill me or something?

The engine turned off, the lights turned off, two people got out and walked right past me, mumbling to each other as they went into the house. As soon as their door closed, I could hear Toad laughing his ass off down the street.

"Whoooo! Now that's fucking hilarious!" He kept laughing, now joined by Phil.

I took off running from the house and by the time I caught up to them I was laughing, too. We laughed ourselves silly, turning around every so often to look for imaginary cop cars.

A few more minutes and we were in front of Tom's house. Toad opened the duffle bag and we first took care of everything that would be silent. We all took our cans of shaving cream and went to town. Toad filled up the entire mailbox with his can. Phil and I drew all over every window we could find, whether it was on the house or a car.

We then broke out the toilet paper. Thirty-six rolls was an over-calculation but we used it all anyway. They had two big trees in front of the house and one toward the side. Halfway through teepeeing the trees and bushes, a truck drove our way.

Toad spotted it and for the first time in his life used a whisper. "You guys! Get down! Get down! Take cover!"

The truck slowed down to a stop in front of the house and we could hear laughter coming from inside before it drove away.

After the truck was gone, Phil took out the toothpaste and squirted it in all of the door handles of the cars in the driveway. A nasty trick, but the guy did help throw my old skateboard—make that Wes's old board—into the sewer. He must have done something bad to Phil back in junior high because Phil was enjoying himself immensely. A devilish grin peeked out from under the brim of his baseball cap. Toad had a strong arm and actually managed to throw a couple of rolls completely over the two-story house.

"You should join the football team!"

Phil joined in, "Yeah, you're like a quarterback superstar!"

Toad glared at us.

Finally it was time for the eggs. It was super-loud when the eggs hit the front door. It echoed. I thought I was going to die laughing when Toad hit the porch light with one and it made a loud metal CLANG! We took off running after that. I could barely run I was laughing so hard. I even got a cramp in my side. We got down the block and hid.

It looked ghostlike from a distance, like something out of a horror movie. The white streams hanging from the trees swayed silently in the nighttime breeze. It was eerie.

We sat there proud of our work but somehow it didn't seem like enough. On our way home we found a payphone. We called and ordered pizzas to the house from two different pizza joints. Then we ordered a cab.

Chapter 8: The Second Sweater Party

I spent the night at Phil's, and when I got home the next morning I found my father outside stacking firewood. He was mad and he lectured me about coming home too late and that we had things to do around the yard.

"I bust my ass all week at work, putting a roof over your head, and the last thing I want to do on my weekends is bust my ass more getting all the chores done by myself!"

Needless to say, I quickly went into the house, changed into some work clothes and came back out ready to work. My dad had gotten some kind of deal from a friend on some firewood that had just been brought down from the mountains. They must have dropped it off earlier in the morning. I had to take every piece from the street and move it into a neatly organized stack in our backyard.

I knew that we really wouldn't start work on the half-pipe until spring, but I was careful not to stack the wood where it would be going. I didn't want to do anything to postpone its construction.

My dad settled down about halfway through the firewood being stacked, and we started talking about the half-pipe and what it would take to finish it. I could tell in his own way he was excited to build it. The challenge of something that different intrigued him. After we finished, I showed him some pictures of Christian Hosoi in *Thrasher* soaring high above a half-pipe. I informed my dad how he was the champion of air and that no one else could get as high.

Phil and Toad came by and grabbed their skateboards. I guess Toad had never gone home the night before. If he didn't have to be home, he wouldn't be. I don't think he liked his home life much. He spent as much time away from there as he could.

We agreed to meet up after dinner so Phil's stepdad could give us a ride to the party. By now I was pondering who would show up. I decided I wanted to look my best. I skated off to the mall in an attempt to find a Cure T-shirt.

It was a search in futility. The kind of music I was into and the bands I now liked were nowhere to be found in my suburban mall. I asked the clerk at one store if they had any Cure shirts and he literally laughed at me.

"No, man. You'll have to go somewhere else to find something like that."

Instead I ended up buying a black Tony Hawk shirt at the skate shop. It was black with a blue hawk head on it. I figured I'd wear it at the party.

I tried to make my hair stand up as best I could. I used a ton of some Aqua Net I found in the bathroom cabinet. I wanted a Robert Smith look, but ended up with a John Lydon look. The only thing was that I didn't know who John Lydon was.

"You're not going out like that, are you?" my dad asked.

I was hoping to get out the door before he saw me. I told him I was going to my friend's party and not to worry because I'd be the most normal-looking guy there.

As I skated over to Phil's, I thought about my parents and how on the weekends all they did was sit and watch TV. I tried to imagine a younger 1960s version of them at house parties, getting drunk, and making noise. My father with greasy hair, a suit and a martini like in an old movie, and my mom with a big hairdo.

I was excited for this second party. Toad, Phil, and I were probably going to get the hero's treatment because of the job they had done bragging to everyone about our teepee adventure. I had already received a phone call and praise from Rob and Rachel earlier in the day.

When I got to Phil's house we tried to get Toad to borrow one of Phil's shirts since he was still wearing the same clothes he had warn the past few days. Toad insisted he was more punk rock than us because he didn't care about stuff and that guys who change their shirts all the time were pussies.

Phil's stepdad dropped us off about a block away from the party so we didn't have to be embarrassed about having been dropped off. The walk up to the house was chilly.

Once we got in front of Rob and Rachel's, we stopped for a second. Phil, Toad, and I stood there looking at the unassuming, quiet house in front of us.

"I swear I'm not gonna get as drunk as last time," Toad said. "And I'm getting laid!"

I'd just be happy not to end the night in the back of another police car.

We walked up to the door, which Rachel opened a crack. She peered out at us.

"None of you are wearing sweaters. I'm not letting you in."

We stood there.

"C'mon, it's cold," Phil said.

"Then I guess you should have worn your Morrissey sweater, shouldn't you?" she said. I tried to think of something clever to say but as usual I didn't have anything. Toad spoke up while pushing his way inside.

"Guys who wear sweaters are pussies!"

And we were inside.

"I'm not giving you guys a drop to drink! This is, after all, the first official Sweater Party and you have to pay homage to Morrissey or The Smiths to get in," she over-annunciated.

"Morrissey?" Toad shrugged. He looked almost confused.

"From The Smiths," Rachel quipped.

Phil interrupted, "We did the best teepee job on a jock bastard since 1978!"

She laughed.

"I guess you earned *a* drink. Who got teepeed in '78?" she asked.

Phil shrugged. "I don't know."

Rob rushed over to greet us. We must have been the first people to get to the party because it was empty *and* he was giving us his full attention. He brought us into the kitchen and fixed us drinks. He handed me a pink bottle of Boone's. It was pretty good. Toad wouldn't drink it. He told me Boone's is for pussies and instead fixed himself a jack and coke. Phil had a beer.

We sat in the TV room and Rachel excitedly showed us the most recent additions to her videotape of *120 Minutes*. Lightning Seeds, Candy Flip, The Charlatans—but the best was a video from a band called Nitzer Ebb. It was just so cool. We sat and talked for a while, every now and then being interrupted by small groups of people coming in the front door.

Phil was bragging about the status of the teepeed house.

"So we skated by this afternoon and the entire mess, everything we did, was gone! It was all gone! Can you believe that? It looked like we'd never even been there."

"I wonder if they woke up early and cleaned it all up or if they cleaned it up last night?" Rob asked, before getting up to answer another knock at the door.

"They had to be pissed! But I was fucking bummed out when we got there and it was all gone, I'll tell you that," Toad said.

More people were filing in and it was getting too hard to see and hear the TV, so we turned it off and started playing music. Rob had made a mix tape earlier in the day so people wouldn't spend the whole night fighting over what to play. He made sure to include a number of Morrissey and Smiths songs to keep Rachel happy.

I was disappointed when Sarah came in alone. She said that Elizabeth might show up later but was vague about it. As she was talking about it, I was positive she shot me a weird look. Phil was happy that the girl he liked had shown up and he immediately started talking with her about last night's teepee adventure. He made sure to cover every detail.

When Rachel made Sarah a drink, I made the mistake of joking with Sarah not to get as drunk as last time.

"What are you talking about? I wasn't that drunk," she said while glancing around to see who might be in earshot.

I let it slide and went into the other room. I sat down and started talking to these deathrock guys from some other school. I guess they had met Rob somewhere along the way. They had really cool style. They wore all black and one was wearing a T-shirt for a band called Christian Death. They wore a ton of eyeliner and one of them had a long black skirt over his pants and boots. They told me more about Skinny Puppy and Nitzer Ebb. They talked about how this guy Ogre was from Canada and how Nitzer Ebb was from overseas and how they thought American music sucked. Halfway through the conversation I realized I was getting tipsy. I had never felt that way before—it was like a warm haze. I had finished one bottle of Boone's.

It felt like the party was off to a good start. Phil had disappeared off somewhere with Sarah, and Toad wasn't getting himself into too much trouble. Every time I'd see Toad, he was bragging to a new group of people about the details of what we had done the night before. He would call me over and have me confirm the tall tale he was feeding them. As his drinking continued, his tale got taller and taller. There was a version where he ran from the cops and ditched them by climbing over a fence and a version where he even slashed all of the tires on one of the cars.

One of the times he called me over to confirm, I didn't mind going because he was with a group of girls I had never seen before. They were all cute. One of them looked like Siouxsie Sioux. He was bragging about the story and I just kept nodding yes as he continued. Then the doorbell rang again. Rachel squealed when she opened the door and Elizabeth walked in. And Elizabeth wasn't alone.

She was with some new guy I had never seen before. He was tall, feminine, and very good-looking. His hair was teased perfectly in a Robert Smith kind of way—the way I tried earlier to get my hair but failed. He had pointy boots with buckles and was wearing make-up.

The girls who were listening to Toad looked over and began talking amongst themselves. They were obviously excited that this guy had just walked in. He looked around the room as Rachel gave Elizabeth a hug and pulled her inside. Elizabeth was wearing a leather jacket that appeared to be too big for her. I realized it was probably his. It also dawned on me that they were there *together*, not just together.

The black gooey decay started filling my insides again. As the sinking feeling took over, I asked one of the girls who the guy was.

"That's Mark. He goes to our school and he's so fucking hot. Everyone is in love with him. I don't know who the girl is though, lucky tramp."

After hearing those words, she didn't seem as cute to me anymore. Suddenly, none of them seemed attractive. They all seemed lame. The entire party seemed lame. Everything was lame. Now I knew what that look from Sarah earlier had been about. Sarah... I'd find her and she could tell me what was going on. Like I needed her to tell me. But I wanted details on why I was about to feel bad for myself.

It was like driving by a car wreck. You know it's going to bother you. You know it will be ugly, but you want to see it anyway. For Elizabeth, I was going to force myself to look, no matter what it did to my heart. The air was once again stolen from me and before I could escape, Elizabeth and the *new* guy found their way over to us.

The girls from the other school were saying hi to him while Elizabeth tried to give me a warm hello. The look on my face betrayed me. She could tell how I was feeling. I think anyone at the party could have guessed.

"Hey, this is Mark," she said.

He reached out to shake my hand. I then reached down and shook his hand. I really wished I wouldn't have. I really wished I hadn't shaken that hand. Instead, I should have freaked out and trashed the place. But I was caught off guard. I just reached down and shook his hand like the jackass I was. Then they were off into the kitchen for a drink.

Toad went to grab me another drink while the girls from the other school told me I'd been rude to Mark.

"Sorry, man. All that's left is beer, but you need it." He handed it to me and I took a big swig.

"Besides, you don't want to be seen drinking that pink wine shit!"

The beer tasted bitter and metallic compared to what I just had been drinking. But it didn't matter. I took another big swig and went off to find Phil. Toad stopped me. He spoke quietly in my ear.

"Dude, you cool?"

"It's just that Elizabeth is here with that guy."

"Forget it, dude. This party is crawling with hot chicks!"

That was Toad for you. That was Toad logic. I thanked him but figured I'd rather go find Phil and Sarah.

The party had gotten really crowded. There were a lot of people I didn't recognize and there were people I knew from the last party. The last party… This was nothing like the last party. The last one had been peaceful and great. We all hung out together. Tonight, suddenly, I was alone.

Maybe I'd been expecting too much. Maybe hoping this night would be like that last one was expecting too much? I just wanted it to be silent. I wanted it to be warm and I wanted to be lost out in that field behind the house. I wanted to see Elizabeth under that bluish night again.

Instead, I was stuck in that house. It was crowded with blank faces, thick with smoke, the air polluted with voices, conversations and music. The party was a big cloud hanging over my senses. Confusing. I set down what was left of the beer in some planter and headed upstairs, which was off limits to everyone.

I figured maybe I could find Sarah and Phil up there. As I walked by the bathroom door, I heard someone puking inside. Then I found a closed door. I knocked lightly and heard no voices. I cracked the door open and looked inside.

It was Rachel's room. I had never seen it before. It was very soft, for lack of a better term that wouldn't offend Toad. The walls were covered with the evidence of her life: posters of her favorite bands and a couple of nicely framed black and white photographs that looked like they were from a museum or something. There was a dresser with a big mirror on the top of it and a lit candle.

The room seemed so warm. Along the edges of the mirror were photographs of Rachel with the others. There were pictures of her and Rob when they were very small. They looked like funny kids with Sesame Street wardrobes and shaggy heads. Phil and Toad were in a couple of the photos, but mostly they were of Rob, Rachel, Elizabeth, and Sarah.

There were pictures of them at a concert. They were all really made-up. From the pictures, it looked like Rob used to dress a lot crazier. He even had some make-up on in one photo, which didn't really seem like him now. And Elizabeth looked much happier in the pictures, younger or maybe more carefree. I was tempted to take one of the photos with her in it but decided that would have been too creepy. I couldn't help being fascinated with the pictures Rachel had stuck up in that mirror. I also couldn't help but feel a little jealous that I wasn't in any of them. With that haunting me, I decided I better get out of her room.

I moved down the hall to a second door. Knocking softly, I heard Phil's muffled voice.

"Yeah, what's up?" he said through the door.

I cracked it open and poked my head inside. In front of me, lying on the floor entangled with each other, were Phil and Sarah. This must have been Rob's room and they both looked embarrassed. I probably looked more embarrassed than they did, and yet my quest for the truth about Elizabeth fueled me forward.

"Hey, close the door behind you, man," Phil said.

I shut the door and sat down.

"Dude, what's up?" Phil asked.

At least he could tell something was bothering me. I told them about how Elizabeth had just shown up and that I just met Mark.

"I was afraid this would happen tonight. I'm so sorry. I should have warned you, but I just couldn't bring myself to tell you. They met a couple of weeks ago. They've been together a lot, but he has been really nice to her," Sarah sheepishly told me.

"That doesn't make me feel much better about it," I said.

"You should be happy that she has something that's making her happy. She's been going through some tough shit lately. And if you really like her, you would at least be glad she's happier than she has been!"

I didn't feel like arguing with Sarah about this. And I didn't like the fact that she was probably right. Everything was making me feel like a jackass, every bit of it. Now I was feeling awkward for interrupting Phil and Sarah.

"I'm gonna go back downstairs," I said.

"Is everything cool?" Phil asked. I didn't know what he meant.

"What do you mean?" I asked.

"Are we cool?" he said.

I realized he felt bad about the situation.

"Yeah, of course! We're cool."

I felt like I had to get away. I hurried back downstairs.

I was in a weird mood when I got downstairs. I was just about to start feeling sorry for myself when I ran into a familiar face. It was Steve. The guy who gave me the Skinny Puppy tape. He was standing at the foot of the stairs with some friends, drinking beer. He wore the same black trench coat and boots.

His friends were large punk guys with lots of spikes and leather. If they weren't standing with him, I would have been really intimidated by them. He introduced me—one was named Gabo and the other was Mikey.

"Hey, did you check out that tape I gave you?" he asked.

"Yeah, it's really fucking great," I said. A small exaggeration, it was actually totally out there and I was having some trouble getting into it. We talked for the next half hour. He told his friends how he always saw me around and they talked about other people I didn't know and music I didn't know, either. They also talked about getting drunk a lot. These guys were the real deal. Hardcore. I felt more legitimate just standing there with them.

A Morrissey song came on the stereo and the four of us laughed when some skater guy stumbled through the room trying to change the stereo. He fell down, spilling his beer, and everyone cheered. I was just starting to enjoy myself again when I saw Rachel dart by with tears in her eyes. She looked really upset. Elizabeth followed her into the kitchen. Gabo muttered something about chicks always crying at parties as I followed them into the kitchen.

It was so uncomfortable in the kitchen that other people were fleeing into the front room.

"What's going on? Are you all right?" I asked.

"Don't worry about it," Elizabeth said. "Can you just go and find Sarah?"

But that wasn't good enough. I was her friend now, and I wanted to know what was going on.

"I want to know what's wrong," I insisted. Elizabeth gave me a "mind your own business" look when Rachel raised her head and pointed toward the front of the house.

"Brad and his friends just showed up. I guess somehow they got hold of one of Rob's flyers," she said, starting to weep. I walked up to the front of the house and saw that Rob was outside facing Brad Thompson and two of his friends. It looked like Rob was preventing them from coming inside. I overheard a little of their conversation.

"Yeah, we're cool with you guys. Why aren't you being cool with us?"

"My sister would feel uncomfortable with you here, that's why. It has nothing to do with anyone else."

"Dude, you're usually cool. What's up?"

I headed back into the kitchen. Toad was trying to figure out what was wrong.

"Dude, what's up with this party? Everyone's so depressed. Fuck!"

With that, Elizabeth asked him to go find Sarah. I told him to check upstairs. He grabbed another beer and took off upstairs, muttering to himself, "It's the music you guys play. Fuck, it's so depressing."

Mark came into the kitchen. I really didn't want to see him at the moment.

"Is everything okay?" he asked.

Elizabeth walked over and started quietly informing him of the situation. Tears kept streaming down Rachel's face, so I went over to her.

"Rob's not going to let those assholes in the party, so try not to worry about it," I said.

"I know," she said. "It's just that, well, forget about it."

I grew more agitated.

"I'm sick of always forgetting about it. I want you to tell me what's wrong so I can help."

"There's not really anything you can do. I'll just go upstairs and calm down a bit," she said. I turned and looked at Elizabeth and her new boyfriend.

"Can I talk to her alone for a minute?" I asked. Elizabeth gave me a weird look but they walked out into the front room. I leaned on the counter next to Rachel. Words just started pouring from her mouth.

"You know how everyone was talking about all of those rumors after Halloween? Some of them weren't rumors. I just. I never had guys like that like me. The popular guys never liked the girls like me. He was acting so nice. I just figured that maybe he was different from the others. Maybe he understood us more," she said.

"So you did get together with him that night?" I asked, trying to contain my disgust and shock.

With more tears about to flow, she nodded yes. "I was pretty buzzed and he was acting really sweet and it seemed like we might have had something. We got a ride home with him and his friends. And I...hung out with him. I didn't hear from him the rest of the weekend. Then when I got to school that Monday he acted as if nothing had happened. When I cornered him on it, he said that I was 'hot and good for it,' but that no one would understand why he would be with a girl like me."

Anger shot through me, my blood turning blacker than it had ever been before. Poisoned and angry, I started toward the front door. Phil and Sarah were coming down the stairs. "What's going on?" Phil asked. I ignored him.

"Where are you going?" Rachel asked me with a kind of whine. "Don't go out there. Don't." I was already halfway out the front door.

Rob was still out front trying to smooth things over. He was talking to Brad, who was facing him in the front yard. I brushed past Rob and unloaded as hard as I could on the middle of Brad's face. I felt his nose give way under my lead knuckles. Something crunched. I kept hitting. My hand felt wet. I kept hitting. Soon we were down on the ground and I don't remember much else. I just kept punching.

Moments passed and a combination of people pulled me off him. I was still engulfed in rage and he was now on the ground clutching his bleeding face. A huge group of people came outside to watch. Rob and the two friends helped a staggering Brad into their truck.

As they drove away, Rob turned and gave me a look. I couldn't tell if he was happy or pissed. All of a sudden it was cold outside. My knuckles started to sting. I turned around to find I was being watched by the group of people the way you'd look at an ugly animal at the zoo.

"Go back in the house, nothing else to see!" Rob told them, agitated.

A few guys shouted congratulatory remarks toward me as they headed back inside. The two figures remaining on the porch were those of Rachel and Elizabeth. They were still looking at me. I couldn't figure out what the looks on either of their faces meant. Phil and Toad were on their way over to congratulate me when Rob asked them to go back inside.

"We need to talk for a second," he told them.

Everyone headed back inside except for Rachel, who watched from the porch as Rob and I walked out into the middle of the deserted suburban street.

"There had to be a better way of dealing with him. You lost your cool and there had to be a better way of dealing with things!"

He sounded like someone's dad.

"When someone's fucking with one of my friends I tend to lose my cool," I said. Wow. That really didn't sound like me.

I continued, "Sometimes situations take actions, not words."

I was sounding more and more like the kind of kid who'd wear one of the punk band patches sewn onto Phil's hoodie instead of the terrified victim from Great Leaders class. Only part of Rob's face was illuminated by the streetlight. He stared at me for a moment. I was starting to worry about what he'd say next. He patted me on the shoulder.

"Thanks for looking out for my sister, man."

He walked back inside. I stood there in the street with Rachel looking back at me from the porch. It had gotten really cold outside. I realized I could see my breath and then I looked down to find clumps of wet grass and mud stuck to my pants and shirt. My hands were covered in a mix of blood and dirt. My right hand was starting to hurt. Damn. It hurt bad.

Rachel finally spoke.

"What were you thinking? You could have been hurt! Do you realize how they're going to be at school now?"

I didn't know what to say. As usual, I was at a loss for the right words. At the end of the previous Sweater Party I had felt free and beautiful. I couldn't have ended this one feeling more different. I felt cold, dirty, and a little older.

When we got back inside, the party was back to normal. People were enjoying themselves again. For me, the entire world had stopped when I went out there and finally stood up for something. But the truth was that some people at the party didn't even see, know, or care about it.

Phil came over.

"I think you did the right thing, man. That kicked ass."

He was excited. He said he wished he would have done the same thing. He also said that if anything went down at school he'd watch my back.

I wasn't sure what Elizabeth thought of everything and I wouldn't get the chance, because soon after I came back inside she left with Mark, wearing his cool leather jacket and not looking back. She didn't say goodbye to me. Not that she ever did.

The party thinned out. Most people left after the beer ran out. Rachel and Sarah went into the freezer and grabbed a bag of frozen peas to put on my hand. It felt like they were looking at me differently. Had I changed? Had something changed?

Rob and Rachel made hot chocolate with some Baileys in it and we ended the night sitting on the porch watching the still street in front of us. Phil had his arm around Sarah, which was cool. She sometimes annoyed me, but he liked her so I was happy for him. Toad was passed out on the couch inside, so we joked with Rachel and Rob that they had just inherited Toad for the rest of the weekend.

Light snowflakes were falling, little flecks of white against the gray black night. The season had changed and something within me along with it.

Chapter 9: Combat Boots

I was never sure why, but for some reason we kept some of my uncle's things, including a big green bag filled with his old army clothes, in the attic of my house. Recently, I'd started to raid the bag for cool clothes to wear. He had a pair of steel-toe combat boots. I had been eyeing them for a while, trying to work up the courage to wear them out in public. I'd also been trying to gather the courage to wear them in front of my parents.

The only people they saw wearing boots were hardcore punks and skinheads on the news, and I'm sure they didn't want me being associated with either. I tried, on many occasions, to explain to them that there was a difference between skinheads and punks but they couldn't understand what I was talking about, and they feared that other people couldn't see the difference, either.

I didn't give these concerns a second guess as I laced up the boots and pulled them on the Monday after the party. Phil and Toad did a good job of convincing me there would be trouble at school after what I did to Brad Thompson. I knew it would be smart to be wearing some good boots in case I got jumped.

"They're gonna want payback, man!" Toad kept saying.

Maybe he was right. Toad had a lot more experience with fights than I did.

"Whatever happens, I got your back, man," Phil reassured me.

"You couldn't punch your way out of a wet paper bag," Toad told him.

Whether or not that was true, I was glad to have his support.

I thought that I'd find new graffiti written on my locker. To my surprise, there was nothing.

I ran into Rachel and Phil, and they seemed normal. So far everything was normal. I was glad but anxious, waiting for the other shoe to drop.

When I got to gym, the teacher was pissed because I didn't have gym shoes and couldn't work out. I forgot that morning that I'd need to take shoes for gym. For the entire class, I sat watching the others run back and forth on the basketball court and pondered how bad my grade would be this semester. After class, Wes walked over to me in the locker room. An unusual move, as we normally just avoided each other.

"I heard what happened, man," he said in a disapproving voice.

"Yeah, well, he shouldn't have come by the party. He knew he wasn't welcome there," I said.

"Yeah, maybe you're right. But there's a group of guys from the football team going around telling everyone how you jumped Brad because there were more of you than them. They said they're going to teach you a lesson."

I studied him for a second.

"What happened to you, man?"

"Nothing happened to me," he said. "Things are just different here."

I didn't care to argue with him there in the locker room.

"Well, see you around, man."

Frustration erupted on Wes's face.

"I'm trying to warn you to chill out so nothing else happens!"

"I'm standing up for something—you even remember what that's like?" I asked him. Then I walked away, as I didn't care to hear his response.

By lunch, the talk was everywhere about the fight over the weekend. I guess Brad had a black eye and scratches on his face. People kept asking him what happened and he would tell them that he got jumped by skaters. His two friends kept their mouths shut about what really happened.

In art class, Chad kept asking to hear details about the fight while Elizabeth continued ignoring me. He kept saying how he wished he'd been at the party and she kept staring down at her desk.

I wanted her to say something. I wanted her to be glad that I stood up for her friend or at the very least act like I was there. When class was over and she was leaving, she turned around and gave me a somber look. I was sure she was about to say something but she didn't.

Tom, whom we'd teepeed over the weekend, was in my English class. He kept looking over at me during the course of the class. Finally, I spoke.

"What are you looking at?"

"You're gonna get your ass kicked!" he said.

I was trying to figure out if they were going to kick my ass over what had happened with Brad, or the teepee job. I guess it didn't really matter. A few weeks ago, I would have been scared to death that something was going to happen. But now I just didn't care. Taking their shit for all of that time was worse than getting beat up, so it didn't matter.

"The other guys saw your boots, you fucking freak, so we're *all* gonna kick your ass," he said.

The boots? I thought. They just needed an excuse. It wasn't me punching out Brad, or the teepeeing; it was something that didn't even make sense. I didn't like the sound of it. If I was going to get my ass kicked, I wanted it to be for something real.

After class, he was joined by three other guys. They were large and wore school colors. As I walked down the hall, I felt them following. Every now and then more guys joined them. Thanks to all the team jerseys, they were beginning to look like a small green-and-yellow-trimmed army.

I was getting my stuff out of my locker when Rachel showed up with Rob, Phil, and Sarah. Rachel looked upset.

"We're giving you a ride home!" Rachel commanded.

From over her shoulder, I could see the looming mass of green-and-yellow letter jackets and jerseys. They were standing with Brad Thompson and looking my way.

"I told you there had to be a better way of dealing with all of this," Rob said.

"C'mon, we're giving you a ride home today," Rachel insisted again.

I looked at the faces of Rob, Sarah, and Phil. They were scared.

"Where's Toad?" I asked.

They didn't know.

"Why?" asked Rob.

"Because I'm walking home and I know he can fight," I said.

Disappointment filled their faces, disappointment that I wasn't going to ride with them, or that for once I was acting more like Toad than like them.

"What the hell are you thinking? Just get a ride with us today and this will all blow over!" Rob said.

"I don't care if it blows over! I'm tired of this! Aren't you tired? So they kick my ass. I don't give a fuck!"

Toad walked up, looking at the crowd.

"What the fuck is going on?" he asked.

I told Toad what was happening and that I was ready to start walking home. We told the others not to worry and to just go home, that we'd talk to them later. Reluctantly they agreed, but not before Phil spoke up.

"It's a nice day today. Maybe I feel like walking home, too!" He was smiling nervously.

And we were off.

Other students watched in silent understanding of what was going on. How the faculty couldn't tell was beyond me. There was definitely something in the air, ominous, informing the school of the coming fight.

I felt good walking out of the school with Toad and Phil backing me up. They were good friends. But the warm feeling quickly disappeared when I saw that Wes was with the group of jocks that were following us. We walked for a couple of blocks until they ironically caught up to us on Oakwood Drive. The pack sped up to cut us off. It seriously looked like half the football team without their pads and helmets.

Our path was now blocked and they waited. They waited for me to do something. Toad, Phil, and I were silent until Wes forced his way through the crowd. He walked over to me.

"Dude, just back down and walk away. Walk away. Eventually they'll forget about it."

Toad and Phil tensed up behind me.

"Maybe *we're* not forgetting about it!" Toad said.

Well put. Phil was silent. He looked worried, his eyes shifting back and forth, looking at the odds. I looked over at the group of guys. I didn't even know who any of them were, until I saw Brad. His face was pretty beat-up. He didn't look as defiant as he used to look. Once I saw him, the rage came back to me. I could feel it starting to course through my blood. I shoved Wes out of the way and I pointed at Brad.

"If you ever fuck with one of my friends again, none of these guys will be able to stop me from kicking your ass!"

"You better watch your mouth!" one of the faceless jocks barked from the crowd.

I shouted again, louder, "Did you hear me?" I didn't plan any of these words—they were just coming out. He looked at me with a mix of anger and embarrassment. I shouted again, still pointing my finger in rage.

"Did you hear me?"

He stood there saying nothing. I looked at all the others.

"Then we have nothing else to say! You want to kick my ass? Do it! Kick my fucking ass! I don't fucking care anymore!"

The group didn't know what to do. I don't think they expected me to act like this. I didn't expect me to act like this. It was like someone else was speaking through my mouth—someone a little crazy, foaming at the mouth and all that.

I stood facing Brad for a few more seconds. Nothing happened. Once I didn't care anymore, they had lost the only weapon they had. The weapon of fear.

It was over. They had pushed and pushed until it was over. Whatever mistrust, hate, or lack of understanding that ran between all of the groups at my school, this was as far as it could go.

The large group of jocks dispersed and we all went our separate ways. It's not that I had some magic solution, did the right thing, and everything just worked out. For the rest of the year there were still comments made, small dramas and tensions between us. But nothing like it had been. I never had another run-in with Brad Thompson.

I took the combat boots off when I got home so Phil, Toad, and I could go skate.

Elizabeth transferred to the school where Mark, the boyfriend, went. I found out from Sarah that she was having problems at home, so she'd moved in with an older sister in another part of town and that's how she ended up at the other school.

The rest of the school year continued on without her. Rob, Rachel, Toad, Phil, and I grew much closer. They were my friends now, not just the members of the Freak Table.

There wasn't another Sweater Party for well over a year.

Chapter 10: The Nightclub

I spent most of the summer working on the half-pipe if I wasn't doing anything else. Well, I guess you could call it working on the half-pipe. Another way to put it is that I was working on the ground. We had to make sure the ground was completely level where the ramp was going, so I had to do all of this backbreaking work to get it that way. My dad was definitely the one who oversaw things and put me to work. I'm sure he figured it was good for me. I didn't mind because in the end, when I was finished, I would have an awesome half-pipe.

We had to drill and dig really deep holes for the supports. You can build a ramp without structural supports, but my father would often say that if we were going to do it, we would do it right.

My hair was longer now and successfully stuck up in big clumps of spikes. I wore dark blue nail polish and had some cool-looking skate rags. I finally found that elusive Cure shirt I was looking for and wore it into the ground. I had some black suede Vision Street Wear shoes my mom got me for Christmas. It was safe to say I was looking more like Phil and Toad and less like a Chad or a Brad.

I didn't see Rob and Rachel at all that summer. They went on an extended trip to Europe with their parents. Finding that out made their neighborhood seem even farther from mine. A vacation for people in my neighborhood would be the Grand Canyon—if they were lucky, maybe Disneyland. But Europe? I was lucky if my parents made the annual trip to my grandparents' house.

I guess Rob and Rachel's parents wanted to take one more trip as a family before Rob went off to college. Their parents were also having marital problems and were hoping a trip of that magnitude would help the family. At the end of the summer, they expected to be occupied with getting Rob ready for school. He was going to college somewhere in northern California. The joke was that he was going to come back a surfer.

Rob and I hung out one last time before he was to leave. It was a cloudy summer day with afternoon showers. There's nothing like an afternoon thunderstorm in Colorado. It's like these cold northern winds collide in battle with warm weather from the south and the battleground is the sky above the plains. The lightning and thunder were relentless that afternoon as Rob and I took refuge in Perkin's, drinking coffee.

You can find these chain family restaurants in any city or town, no matter where you are in America. And no matter which one you go to, if there is a smoking section you'll find wayward youth in concert shirts and all-black clothing drinking coffee and smoking cigarettes.

Usually I was with Rob, Rachel, or some combination of those two and others, but this time it was just the two of us. He read through the *Westword*—a free local entertainment paper—and I wrote in a spiral notebook. Rob broke the silence.

"You've gotta do me a favor while I'm away at school. Keep an eye out for Rachel. I mean, I know you would anyway, but I don't mean at school. My parents have not been getting along and I won't be around for her, so if she just seems down or something try to help out, okay?"

Like always, I didn't have a good response. I shrugged.

"Yeah, sure, man."

I reached for my coffee.

"Of course I'll look out for her. *If she'll let me.*"

He laughed. He knew exactly what I meant. Rachel and her friends weren't exactly the kind of girls to pull the damsel-in-distress routine. If anything, they always wanted to figure things out for themselves. He shook my hand, thanked me, and went back to reading the paper. I continued writing random ideas in the notebook I had been carrying around.

Although I hadn't seen her all summer, Elizabeth was still hanging around with Sarah and Rachel. They were a team that stuck together. It didn't matter to them that Elizabeth was off at another school with a boyfriend, or that Sarah spent most of her time with Phil, they were the best of friends.

I didn't see Phil as much that summer because he was always off with Sarah. He wasn't skating as much, so I hung out with Toad a lot more. I was finally getting to understand his world and where he was coming from. He didn't freak me out as much as when we first met. I always hated going to his house though, because someone was always fighting, screaming, or breaking something.

A couple nights before school was going to start, Toad, Phil, and I were skating and ran into Steve, Gabo, and Mikey. They were hanging out in the grocery store parking lot, playing Black Flag from a really crappy car stereo and eating hamburgers from somewhere nearby.

We hung out for a while, trying to pull off tricks on our boards while talking to them. The conversation really set the tone for the way things were, the way things were going, and how some things would never be the same again.

"It's bullshit, man. Bullshit."

Gabo's hawk was in its full glory, he was wearing his leather, which had hundreds of spikes in it, and he was trying to Ollie on my board. I stood there, his audience, trying to take in the pseudo-lecture he was giving.

"You guys got it so easy. Shit, everyone now's got it easy, compared to even a few years ago. People used to jump punkers all the time, man. And now, that shit's not happening anymore, at least not like it used to. And that's a bad fucking sign, man."

Mikey joined in, "Yeah, man. Things are getting more acceptable, right?"

"Fuck yeah, they are. And I'll tell you guys something, especially you pussy little skaters. You may think it's cool people are starting to come around, you may think it's cool jocks aren't trying to jump your asses as much, but I'll tell you something: it's the worst fucking thing that could happen!"

Luckily, Phil interrupted their seriousness by pulling off a cool trick. Even Gabo was impressed.

"That's some nice fucking shit, Phil!" Gabo told him appraisingly. Then Steve spoke from behind the can of soda he was drinking. "Gabo, you sound like somebody's grandpa!"

Everyone laughed, especially Toad.

"Yeah, punk rock grandpa!"

"When I was your age, we couldn't just go buy T-shirts for punk bands, we had to make our own. We wrote everything on our own damn clothes, you spoiled brats!" Gabo croaked in a grandpa-voice. He picked up my skateboard, acting as if it was a cane as he walked with a hunch in circles.

"When I was your age, we had to buzz our own heads, you little fuckers!"

Steve laughed.

"Gabo's gonna make a great grandfather one day!"

"Grandchildren, my ass! I'm dying young like Sid, man."

On our way skating home, Phil, Toad, and I agreed we were kind of annoyed with those older guys. Who did Gabo think he was? Us? Have it easy? We were constantly under the threat of getting jumped, and we were constantly taking shit from people.

I guess what he was saying was that it used to be even worse. And if that was the case, I can't imagine how tough those guys had to be to endure it. I'm not sure Phil gave it a second thought after that night. And I know Toad didn't. But I thought for a while about that night, about the sounds our boards made as we pulled off tricks, and the words that Gabo said.

A month after school started, we found out about this nightclub called Chaos. It was a club that hosted a "modern rock" night on Fridays. They had lost their liquor license, so they were catering to the all-ages crowd. You had to be 16 to get in, so those of us who weren't of age would have to use a school ID and say we were old enough. I didn't have to worry about it, but for Phil's sake we hoped that trick would work.

We heard about the club from some other skater guy at our school. There seemed to be more skaters this year. He showed us a flyer that read, "CHAOS." Phil and I decided that on Friday we would check it out. We were pretty excited. Up until that point, none of us had anywhere to congregate except for the Sweater Parties. So word of the new club spread like wildfire among the freaks.

Phil didn't think his parents would let him go to a "nightclub," so he came over to my place to stay the night and we figured we could walk there with Toad. It felt weird leaving our boards behind, but we didn't want to deal with them once we got into the club. I was glad that the suspension I got for driving without a license was almost over. Soon I'd be able to drive us. Not that walking was all bad; some of our best conversations and adventures happened when we were walking places.

Our walk to the club was filled with this beautiful anticipation. The possibilities in front of us were limitless. We were carefree on that walk; school was as far away as it could be, an entire weekend away. Even better, we were marching into a new unknown where anything was possible.

When we got inside, the place was loud with music and filled with smoke. The crowd was like nothing I had seen before. It was like taking the few freaky people from the Sweater Parties and multiplying them by a large and deviant number. I saw all kinds of people I'd never seen before: punks, wavers, and deathrockers. There weren't too many skaters but a lot of freaks.

There were also skinheads. They seemed much older than us; they were weathered and tough-looking. Phil and I figured it was best for guys our age and size to keep our distance from them. Especially after we saw one jerk who was literally shaking kids down for money. He wasn't as big as the others—but who wanted to piss him off enough that he'd call his friends over? We kept joking he was like a bully in an *Our Gang* movie or something.

I was in awe... This was my first realization of the size of the underground culture that was going on. Sure, I was already into the music and my friends and I did our best, and the two Sweater Parties were filled with people like this, but those parties seemed so much smaller and more innocent. This was something bigger, darker, and more established than us. Looking at the various faces in the crowd, I couldn't help but notice the different factions of the scene.

"New Wave" was already a term that had been thrown out. That was part of the problem for people like Phil, Toad, and me. Punk rock was dead. The New Wave scene was over. Who were we? We were without a place. Looking around at all these new faces, I couldn't help but realize just how small we were in this new big picture. I was distracted from my thoughts when a music video started playing on the gigantic wall of video screens.

I wasn't the only one who stopped in their tracks; everyone in the club stopped what they were doing, becoming transfixed as the video played. It was "Warlock" by Skinny Puppy. The song was haunting and perfect. It was one of the most shocking things I had ever seen. Everyone stared in unison at the wall of video screens. Some were horrified, others laughed out of shock. After the video ended, the DJ went back to playing regular songs without videos.

Sarah and Rachel had just come in and Phil was quick to join them. Luckily for me, Gabo, Steve, and Mikey showed up at the same time, so I stuck to them for a while.

The place was now packed with people and fake fog. Dance club lights were flashing, and the video screens were playing computer animation videos. It was fantastic! Everywhere I turned there were people I had never seen. Even better were all the new girls I'd never seen before. I couldn't believe there were that many cool people around town! Where were they during the day? What schools did they go to? Where did they get their pointy boots, and their studded belts? I was finally among the people I wanted to be around.

I had just finished dancing to "Cuts You Up" by Peter Murphy, when the climate on the dance floor changed suddenly. There was a slight pause, then a scream accompanied by a distinct drumbeat ripped through the club. All the tough-looking punks and skins knocked their way through the crowd on their way to the dance floor. On their way toward me! Some large guy with sideburns knocked into my side as he swung his arms. It was getting rough. The song was "Stigmata" by Ministry, and I was witnessing my first pit.

As soon as I figured out what was going on, I retreated from the dance floor. I was almost knocked down twice just trying to get away. I joined Rachel, Phil, and Sarah at a safe distance and watched the craziness in front of us. The song was loud and fast. The lights flashed, bodies slammed into each other, and there in the middle of it all, grinning from ear to ear, was Toad. I think we were all a little surprised to see him in the midst of the chaos with all the older, tougher guys.

He'd get knocked down and spring back up. One time, a big skinhead in overalls picked him up from the ground, then shoved him really hard, sending him flying into some other guys. Toad was really holding his own—once again he had totally impressed me.

The song ended, the pit broke up, and the DJ played a much more mellow song afterward. It was probably in an effort to keep the club from being torn apart.

"C'mon, you guys. The next time you have to go in with me. Don't be pussies!"

"I don't know, man. Some of those guys are fucking huge!" Phil replied.

I'm glad he said it before I had to.

"You guys would love it, I'm telling you!"

Phil and I were not convinced. We'd just watched some of the toughest guys we had ever seen slamming into each other and knocking each other down—larger-than-life skinheads and guys with Mohawks flying around punching each other.

"It looks way worse on the outside, I swear!"

The walk home was great. The air felt so cool and clean after being in the hot and sweaty club. By the time we were halfway home we were freezing, though. It was getting late because we took our time walking. We talked about the girls we saw there and Toad continued bragging about his adventures in the pit. We probably should have accepted a ride from Rachel and Sarah, but I think we needed the walk just to settle down from our first night at a real club.

School wasn't as bad now. Since it was no longer the only place we had to socialize, it just didn't seem as bad. Whatever happened at school didn't matter so much because we knew that the weekend would come and we could go to Chaos. We didn't have to get along with the people at school because we were getting along with an entirely different group of people now. We had an outlet through which to be ourselves. For about a month, we went to the club every Friday. It was our church, a holy place where nothing bad could happen. But that would change.

It was Friday afternoon and Phil and I had survived another week of our crappy school. We got together to work on the half-pipe and ended up skating. This happened often. We'd get together with every intention of working on the half-pipe, then get distracted talking about tricks to try and pull off. We even used some wood from the half-pipe project to build a crude launch ramp, which we drug out into the street in front of the house.

We took turns trying to launch, spin, and land. Phil landed wrong and ate shit so we decided to call it quits for the day. He was so sore he decided to get a ride with Sarah and Rachel to the club later instead of walking with Toad and I. The girls were going early to meet up with some new friends from Elizabeth's school, which to me meant I might get to see Elizabeth.

Phil limped home and I decided it was time to start getting ready. I wanted to look as good as possible in case Elizabeth showed up. I knew she had a boyfriend but it had been a long time since I'd seen her, so at the very least I wanted to look cool. I spiked my hair up as large and out of control as possible. I was able to find black lipstick at a local drugstore because it was so close to Halloween. I decided I was going to brave wearing it. Toad walked in as I was putting it on and he gave me one of his most disgusted looks.

"What the fuck are you doing?"

"You're one to talk, with your dirty-ass green hair."

Toad continued to look at me disapprovingly. From his reaction, I thought it best to sneak out the back door quietly, as to not traumatize my parents. We made our way through the backyard, careful not to kick anything over and make any noise.

As I opened the gate, Toad questioned me again quietly.

"You're not really gonna wear that shit, are you?"

Toad wasn't joking around as much as he used to. Back when we first met, he would have joked and teased me about the lipstick. But, now just the questions. Not even with a sense of sarcasm. I figured things must have gotten worse at home for him.

I couldn't believe I had to defend my actions to him of all people.

"Yeah, man. Of course I am. Who cares?"

He shrugged, changed the subject, and we were on our way. We stopped by the mall on the way to the club. It was crowded with other people who we could tell were on their way to Chaos. There were the usual suburban families pushing strollers, and every now and then you'd see blue or green hair, combat boots, and a leather jacket. It was a funny sight.

Toad and I pretended we were zombies from *Dawn of the Dead* as we made our way to the food court.

"Hey, man, can you spot me for a slice? I don't think I'll have enough for cover if I eat pizza."

I thought about Toad saving what little money he had to get into the club.

"Yeah, I can spot you, man."

We got to the club early. I guess we always did. Rachel and the others would always show up late. She once said that they had to make their "club entrance."

"We need to stroll in fashionably late so everyone can notice our arrival," she said.

Toad was already over in the corner where the pits usually would start. I didn't want to go over there because that was where the skins would hang out. He seemed to be getting along with them okay so he could go over and hang out without any trouble.

I was left to sit in the booth alone, drinking a coke and pretending to have purpose. It felt just like the concession stand at the high school dance, or like the first Sweater Party when I was the wallflower. They played a video—by Alien Sex Fiend—that was cool. I had heard Steve talking about them a few weeks before. At least the club was playing some cool videos.

After a few more songs, Toad came over to me looking serious.

"Keep your guard up tonight, man." He glanced around.

"All those guys are really wound up bad. I guess some friend of theirs got shot with a shotgun up in the mountains last weekend and died. So they're all pissed off and looking for trouble. One of the older guys told me, saying I should watch my step in the pit 'cause they're all pissed off and looking for a fight."

Toad was looking so serious as he spoke that I almost didn't recognize him. It was unlike the Toad I'd met the year before. It definitely didn't sound like good news to me, but as more people from other crowds started to show up I didn't think much more about it. Phil and Sarah finally arrived with Rachel and they were all hanging around with those friends from Elizabeth's school. I recognized the three girls who I had met at the Sweater Party last year.

The girl who looked like Siouxie came over and said hello. We talked for a while about bands and music. She was really nice but I couldn't help being distracted by thoughts of when Elizabeth would show up. I really didn't want to be standing there like a jackass all by myself when Elizabeth walked in, so it was nice the Siouxie girl was talking with me. Eventually she got bored with my distracted look, I suppose, and went back to her friends.

Phil was requesting music at the DJ booth with Sarah. His mission to get Fugazi played in the club was still unaccomplished. Rachel was off talking to some guy she had a crush on from the week before.

I was left to watch the video wall by myself again when I felt a light tap on my shoulder. Relieved to have someone to talk to I turned around...to find this bulldog of a skinhead guy I had never seen before. He was about my height, which wasn't too tall, but he had an adult build and a rough look. He was staring me down, right in the face. He just sneered at me. I could smell the whiskey on his breath.

"You look like a fucking woman," he growled.

I didn't have a response.

He leaned in closer, now just inches from my face.

"You look like a fucking woman!"

I shrugged. "Sorry," I said.

He jabbed me in the collarbone really hard with his finger a couple of times, then walked away. I could still smell the whiskey as Phil and Sarah walked up.

"What was that all about?"

We were used to being fucked with everywhere else, but here at the club *and by that guy*? This was different, more serious. These weren't just jock guys in high school.

This skinhead movement was a dark cloud hanging over all of us. And it was a movement that was growing quickly. These guys didn't fuck around—they were the violent and racist type. Toad's recent warning echoed in my head.

Phil asked me again, "What was that all about?"

I didn't want it to get any worse.

"Nothing."

We walked over to tease and talk to Rachel, but the entire time Toad's warning echoed in the back of my mind.

Those worries quickly disappeared when I saw Elizabeth walking in. It had been so long since I'd seen her. As always, she was beautiful.

Her hair was different—It had grown out. She looked good, more healthy and full of life than last year. She was glowing. I was happy she looked good, but I couldn't help lamenting that I'd had nothing to do with it.

It was Mark, of course. He looked pretty much the same as the last time I'd seen him. Fucking perfect. Phil and I had run into him a couple of times over the summer at different places but I always acted like I didn't recognize him. His hair was up perfectly. His clothes were cool. He had on make-up that was flawless, and girls turned their heads with squeals when he walked by.

As the two made their way over to us, I had this uncanny urge to escape. I didn't know why. And then I was saved. I was saved from every uncomfortable thing I had to think about. "Bizarre Love Triangle" came on. The DJ was playing New Order. I had the beginning of that song memorized as well as my own name. I didn't have to make conversation with Mark, I didn't have to feel awkward with Elizabeth, I didn't have to think about that guy telling me I looked like a woman.

Instead I made my way to the crowded dance floor. I guess I didn't realize how popular the song was. I felt in my own way like I was the only one in the world who could have loved it so much. The song was perfect for my mood—the beats, the lyrics, the ironic mix that perfectly blended heartbreak and salvation. It was the soundtrack for the way I was feeling at the moment. I was happy to see her, but sad to see her… The song, the dance floor, the lights—they were consoling me. I was lost in it. People were moving around me. The beats pulsed. It was perfect in a way.

Everything was rushing together in my head. Euphoria. What came next? What would come after? I was in the moment, moving, music pulsing. I was helpless, but I was alive. What could I do? Where would I go from that little spot on the dance floor?

And then I heard it, the distinct clicking of the drum beats, the tribal samples. It was the beginning of "Head Like a Hole" by Nine Inch Nails, a new song that had quickly become a club anthem. A circle cleared almost immediately. Bodies were flailing around taking swings, punching, kicking, pulling, shoving. Pure energy. Pure anger. It was all around us. Toad hopped over the rail and came in swinging. I looked up at the video screens as I tried to back away from the pit. Written over the video image were the words FOR DAN, RIP.

That must have been the guy who'd been killed, the one who was shot. I was getting punched and shoved as I tried to back away from the bedlam. Toad came circling around like a maniac. Everyone in the pit was going crazy. Bodies were flying everywhere. I felt hands and knuckles punch hard into my back. I turned back to find the guy who had confronted me earlier. He grabbed me by the chest of my shirt.

"Show some respect for Dan and get in there!" he shouted.

He threw me like a rag doll into the pit. From there I could feel the rush of everything around me. I was doing my best not to get knocked down. I came around as the circle of bodies moved. Toad swung by grinning, pleased that I had finally joined him. I'm sure he didn't realize it wasn't my choice.

I got knocked down hard. I sprang up as fast as I could, getting shoved really hard into some people on the side of the pit. I turned to find that guy again, the one who had thrown me into the pit. He was bulldogging me. Every time I would come to my feet he would come after me. He was primal. His face looked like a soldier's.

The music was crashing all around us. He grabbed me again and threw me into the wall of people circling us. This time I was pushed back right into him. I thought he was about to kill me but to my surprise he laughed. Then he grabbed me, pushed, and knocked me down again. Among all of these big guys I could barely stay on my feet. Toad was still bouncing around.

I looked over to see that some guy wasn't moshing or slamming but straight out punching. He had grabbed hold of Mark, Elizabeth's boyfriend, and was punching his lights out. In all of the chaos I don't think anyone realized he was just kicking Mark's ass.

Part of me liked seeing Mark humiliated for once. Part of me wanted to let it continue. But instead I grabbed Toad, locked arms with him and did the swinging trick that he had showed me on the soccer fields at the first Sweater Party.

We were swinging, spinning around, and gaining momentum. We shifted our direction; the bigger guys were cursing us. We ran into the guy who was punching Mark as hard as we could; he was knocked to the ground and ate shit. The impact caused Toad and I to fly apart in different directions.

When I came to my feet, the guy was up and coming after me. I could hear him yelling over the music.

"What the fuck! What the fuck!"

Across the pit, Toad was being picked up by one of his big skinhead friends. Mark was stumbling away from the pit, holding his bleeding face. The guy we knocked down had now grabbed hold of me and was about to start punching me when the guy who had thrown me into the pit in the first place knocked him off me. I took the opportunity to retreat as quickly as possible.

For the rest of the song, I hung out on the other edge of the pit behind some people, catching my breath. The song ended and the guy who had thrown me in came over and grabbed me. He spoke in a firm voice.

"My buddy's friend died last week, that's why he's going apeshit. I cooled him down but you and your little faggot friend better take off unless you want trouble."

I nodded. He went back over to the corner where the other guy was now shouting, crying, and being consoled by other tough-looking guys. It was a strange sight. It was sad and scary at the same time. Like watching a wounded bear or something. I decided to take the guy's advice and split.

I went to find Phil to tell him I was leaving. He just figured I was bummed out about Elizabeth and I didn't want to take the time to tell him about what had happened. I knew I had to get out of there. I went to find Toad. It felt like it took forever to find him. He was standing by the big skinhead who had picked him up in the pit and was flirting with a couple of girls. Reluctantly, I walked over.

"Dude, we gotta split. That one guy's pissed at us."

Toad glanced over, then motioned to his new large friend.

"We're cool, man. This guy knows we're cool. He won't let any of the others fuck with us." Toad confidently turned back to the girls he was hitting on.

"Well, I'm gonna go ahead and leave, man."

I was hoping he'd reconsider or follow my lead. Instead he nodded, then reached out to shake my hand.

"Cool, man, I'll see you later."

I was in disbelief… We needed to escape! We needed to stick together! All I was getting from Toad was a handshake?

Astonished, I walked away.

As I was making my way to the front door, I ran into Elizabeth and Rachel, who were just coming from the bathrooms.

"Can you believe that some guy was just punching Mark out there? Trying to beat him up? What is *wrong with* people?" Rachel asked me.

Elizabeth had a handful of paper towels from the bathroom.

"That's crazy. Is he okay?"

"He's fine now. Are you leaving?" Rachel asked.

Before I could even tell them why I had to leave, they were on their way back to Mark with the paper towels for his nose or face or whatever.

I left.

The walk home from the club was lonely. Every time I heard a muscle car drive by with its engine revved up, I thought it was one of those drunk, angry guys looking to kick someone's ass. With that in mind I thought it best to get off the main roads, so I cut through the field. I passed where the mattress and rocks used to be and I thought about a year ago, when Toad was giving us his vampires-and-serial killers story. I ran through the rest of the field. I can really freak myself out sometimes.

As I got to the edge of my neighborhood, I couldn't help being sad about things. It was Friday night and there I was, all alone. Phil had his girl now and Toad was off doing god knew what. It made me miss how things were before the club opened. We'd all just be skating around that time of night.

Then I couldn't help but think of Elizabeth. Once again I did something right. Something cool like help out her lame boyfriend and no one even noticed. Well, except for the drunken skinhead who wanted to kill me.

That led me to thinking about the guy who had been shot with a shotgun. I began to wonder what he'd been doing when he got shot and why. I came to my own conclusion that he was probably doing something wrong. I had these images of winter tree branches, the loud crack of a shotgun in the middle of night, and a guy in a flight jacket bleeding to death in the woods. I wondered if his friends had to drag his limp body to safety.

That train of thought got me feeling sorry for those hard-living guys.

Chapter 11: Downtown

T he next morning, I was awakened by the smell of sausage and biscuits. Being from the south, my dad was addicted to that kind of food and would eat it whenever my mom would let him.

While we were eating Phil called, wanting me to take the bus with him to downtown Denver. He'd heard of this record store that had all kinds of cool T-shirts and CDs for the kinds of bands that we were into. I'd been trying to get him to wait until I had a license and could drive but he really wanted to go.

We grabbed our boards and braved a ride on the bus. I hated the bus. It took forever to get anywhere and we always got dirty looks from people. To get downtown from our neighborhood we had to pass through the neighborhoods that all the gangsters lived in and I wasn't excited about that, either. They always made fun of us if we had our boards.

We didn't know much about downtown, so we got lost a couple times and it took forever to find the place. It was called Dimension Records. It was small but really cool. The walls had these huge posters on them. They had Ministry posters, a Boys Don't Cry poster and a poster for some band called The Birthday Party. All kinds of cool stuff covered the walls. It was a counter-culture museum, this beacon of culture in the middle of cow-town Colorado.

They rented out obscure videos and had bins and bins filled with awesome band T-shirts. Phil bought a red Ministry shirt and I got a Nitzer Ebb shirt. When we bought the shirts, we discovered they were folded and wrapped over old records the store couldn't sell or get rid of. When we got outside and opened them we didn't know what crappy old record we'd find hidden under the T-shirt. We decided the best thing we could do with the old records was to throw them like Frisbees and see who could break one first.

Once our records were smashed into pieces, we sat on a bench and looked through the stuff we bought. A group of punks walked by us and nodded. We recognized them from the club and waved. Then Phil started talking to me in what sounded like a serious tone for him.

"Dude, that Siouxie girl was totally into you last night. I think she tried to talk to you a couple of times."

"We really need to get better with people's names, huh?" I asked him.

He nodded.

"Yeah, we have nicknames for everybody, huh? Listen, you can't spend all your time wishing you had someone you don't. I've seen a couple of rad girls who were into you and you've never done anything about it."

I looked off, pondering a church in the distance, then I looked back at him.

"Well, we all can't just find the girl we like and then get with her. Then spend every hour of every day following her around."

It was a low blow. I'm not even sure where it came from.

"What the fuck is that?" Phil asked. "What do you mean by that?"

I didn't have a response that wouldn't make me sound like a rotten child.

"I'm just saying that everyone you know comes second to Sarah now and sometimes it sucks. It would be cool if you didn't have to check with her first before you made all your plans."

I could tell that I had pissed off Phil.

"If you were with Elizabeth, you would be doing the same thing. Maybe you should try dating someone so you'll know what I'm talking about."

Okay, that was his turn at a low blow. He continued.

"It'd be better then always lamenting over a chick who's got a boyfriend."

All of a sudden, our trip downtown didn't seem so fun or adventurous. The last person I wanted to be this far away from home with was Phil.

"Do you want to get going?" His face was sour.

I nodded.

We skated in silence through the rest of downtown and to the bus stop. We got on the bus and didn't say another word for half the trip home. Even through the gangster part of town where normally we would have talked out of sheer discomfort.

The bus loudly barreled on. Every now and then I'd glance at this old man in a mechanical wheelchair. The seats had been folded up around him, and his chair was strapped to the wall. His head permanently turned to one side. The poor guy had a twisted neck.

As we got into our own neighborhood, Phil and I exchanged a funny look while eyeing all the characters on the bus. We kind of chuckled. The good thing about Phil was that he didn't often get mad, and if he did, he didn't stay mad for long.

"Do I always seem like I'm 'lamenting' over her?"

He nodded. We shook back and forth as the bus hit a bump.

"We don't even have to say her name and I know who you're talking about. That says enough, don't you think?"

He was right.

"All I know is that you kind of...short circuit when she comes around. I'm glad she left school because you got totally more comfortable after she left."

I was embarrassed. I guess I didn't realize how obvious it was. Right there, sitting in the back of that stinking bus, I made a decision. I was now over Elizabeth. She was kind of lame anyway. She never gave me a chance. I assured Phil that I heard what he was trying to tell me and I promised him and myself that I would start looking elsewhere.

Back on familiar turf, we skated to my house and decided to call and check in with Toad about the night before.

"Hey, did you get home okay last night?"

"Sure did, man. No problem."

"Did you get with one of those girls?"

"Yeah, man. It was awesome! Then those skins gave me a ride home and dropped me off... Not bad guys, man."

I didn't know what to think of Toad's last words.

School was flying by. We continued going to the club every Friday for the next few weeks. We didn't even go to the homecoming dance. It was on the same night as Chaos so most of us didn't even entertain the idea of going. Rachel and Sarah went, though. Rachel went with the guy she had met at the club and Phil went with Sarah. They showed up at the club after the dance still dressed in their semi-formal clothes. They kind of stuck out so Toad and I made sure to give Phil a hard time about it. We knew the only reason he went was because Sarah dragged him there.

I was going into the pit more often. I was confident enough to keep trying, but usually just ended up trying to not get my ass kicked. The times I was in the pit seemed like the only times I ever saw Toad at the club. He was always off somewhere else until a pit song came on.

The week after homecoming, Phil and I had something to be really excited about. We had tickets to a show. I was thrilled, but I didn't want to let on to the others that it was my first concert. Phil and I had bought tickets for Skinny Puppy. It was well known in our circles that a Skinny Puppy show was not something to miss.

"It's not just a show, man. It's an experience. This is a band that actually cares about something. They have a message, plus they have all kinds of blood and shit all over the stage!" Steve had told us on a regular basis.

Rachel and Sarah weren't that interested in going to see Skinny Puppy, so Phil and I didn't have a ride. We had to get there somehow and the show was at a venue downtown on South Broadway, so taking the bus home afterward wasn't an option.

Phil was afraid to ask his parents for a ride all the way downtown. He was sure if his mother saw the location and people attending the show, he would be marched off straight to private school.

I knew my parents wouldn't want to drive all the way downtown. If only I had my license… I was so close now.

Phil and I had snuck our boards into school that day and were skating home as we concocted a plan.

"Why don't we just take the bus there? I'm sure once we get to the show, we'll find someone there who can give us a ride back."

"Yeah, but do you really want to get stuck downtown at night if we don't?" "Screw it! That's part of the adventure, right? We're gonna see Skinny Puppy tonight, man!"

"Yeah, I'm so fucking excited."

"Worst comes to worst, we'll get a cab, have him take us a few blocks from where we live and then get out and run so we don't have to pay him!"

I laughed as I popped a curb. "You think that would actually work?"

"I've heard some guys have done it before," Phil said while popping off the same curb. Only he had more air. Damn, he always ollied higher than me.

I settled on my uncle's old green military jacket, skate pants, and a T-shirt for the show. Not that it was any different from my regular garb. I was tempted to put on a bunch of eyeliner but thought about Phil and I trying to bum rides at midnight downtown and figured if we had to walk or something maybe it would be best if I didn't.

The bus ride was an eternity. The sun was going down, and we were anxious to get to the show. A couple of freaky-looking kids got on the bus closer to downtown so we figured we were on the right bus to get to the show

We got off at our stop, walking toward where the venue was supposed to be. Phil assured me he'd been there before but looking around I started to worry. The area was filled with graffiti, trash, and boarded-up buildings. Just as I was sure we were gonna be like victims in a Robocop movie, we came around a corner and found it.

We found ourselves looking at the dilapidated theater; its aged and broken marquee had "Skinny Puppy" spelled out in mismatched black letters. Below that glowing sign was a line of the coolest people in town, a line filled with black eyeliner, pointy boots, silver buckles, and crazy hair. Where did these people come from? Seriously, I didn't recognize any of them. Did they bus in from all the other hick towns on the frontier? Were they normally taking refuge in their basements and bedrooms, only to emerge for shows like this?

Phil and I walked up and down the line a couple of times pretending to look for someone we knew in order to look at all the cute girls. We finally settled and took a place at the end of line. As we waited to get in, we shared drags off cloves with a couple deathrockers in front of us. I'd never had the black cigarettes before and I couldn't help thinking how amazing they were. I also couldn't help thinking that if my mom and dad knew I was smoking they would kill me.

My father enjoyed smoking, but he didn't enjoy the fact that he couldn't quit. He was a proud man, and could usually do anything he put his mind to. Smoking represented something he couldn't beat, and something he didn't want me to start.

Our entrance was delayed because this punker guy in front of us in line was fighting with security about them making him take the spikes out of his leather jacket. He was so pissed off. Security had a pair of pliers and told him unless he yanked the spikes out of his coat he couldn't go in. Compared to that guy, Phil and I got in with no problem.

The theater was old and smelled like it hadn't been kept up very well. The musty smell reminded me of the attic where my uncle's military clothes were kept.

Our first stop was the merch table for T-shirts. Then it was time to make our way through the crowd to get up front. Squeezing our way through the crowd, I couldn't help but feel young amidst all of these people. They looked as if they had been part of the scene forever.

The lights went out and the audience went nuts. As screams and applause filled the air around us there was a flicker on a video screen that took up the back of the stage. The images were digital and surreal, unlike anything I'd seen before. A synthesized hum came over the sound system. It was haunting. And then, with a flash of lights, Ogre took the stage. He was in a kind of fat suit made of plastic, wires, and techno-junk. The audience began to sway and move; the energy was everywhere around us. I had never experienced anything like it.

Like a hurricane forming, a pit developed behind us. I got bumped really hard as the circular crowd grew and grew. It was a storm of bodies. Moments later, I was traveling around the circle myself, getting hit harder than I ever thought I could take. I would get knocked down and some big guy would pick me back up. I could see hints of the video image, of the stage, and of the band. It was this amazing blur streaking through my head.

The pits settled down during the slower songs, and then erupted again when music was fast or hard. I was so tired I finally retreated off to one wall to watch the rest of the show and recover. I didn't know where Phil was and I was worried I wouldn't be able to find him after the show. As I watched the show I couldn't believe we had made it, we were there, it seemed larger than life, we were really in on something secret, something special. The crowd went nuts when it finally ended. I thought they were going to riot when the house lights came back up.

After the show ended, security quickly started kicking us all out, they were literally pushing us out the doors. Luckily Phil spotted me as I spilled out the double doors.

"That was so awesome, man!" he shouted at the top of his lungs. He continued in a smaller yet still excited voice. "What happened? Where did you end up?"

"This big pit started and I got knocked in, and it was like either get killed or go with the flow, so I just went crazy. What a fucking rush!"

"You went in?" Phil was impressed with my bravery. But really, it's not like I had a choice.

"I was in like half the show, except for when all that stuff was going on with the blood. That was crazy!"

Phil and I slightly sobered up from our excited state when we realized we still needed to find a way home. We hung out in front of the show for a while hoping that we'd see a familiar face. We saw lots of people we recognized from Chaos, but none we actually knew. This was beginning to suck. It was cold, late, and it was looking like we didn't have a way back.

We started walking toward the bus stop. We weren't sure if any buses were still running that would take us home, but it was better than just standing there and freezing to death. As we got a couple of blocks away from the theater, I started to realize just how desolate the environment was we were walking through. At that time of night who knew what could happen down there? Phil and I were both so nervous that neither of us brought it up. Instead we talked continuously about the details of the show.

A car drove past and honked. Usually this meant we were about to be fucked with, so both Phil and I jumped about a foot as it passed. The car pulled over to the side of the road just ahead of us.

"Dude, should we turn and go the other way?"

"Yeah, maybe we should take off!"

"Fuck!"

"Wait, look at the bumper sticker!"

It read, "Cocteau Twins," a sure sign we were safe. It was one of us.

Phil and I hurried over to the car and looked inside… It was Mark, Elizabeth's boyfriend. Some other guy was in the passenger seat.

"Hey, you guys need a ride back to the 'burbs?"

I paused and looked at Phil. He could read what was on my mind. Then he gave me a look that said get in the car, you idiot! So we climbed in the back. It was nice and warm. Some good music I'd never heard was playing on the stereo. The guy in the passenger seat reached back to shake our hands.

"Hey, what's up, guys? I've seen you around."

We introduced ourselves. Mark's friend was named Tim, and went to the same school as him in Arvada. As we merged onto the freeway, I couldn't help but glance up at Mark in the driver's seat. His look was flawless as always; I couldn't help but wonder what made him different, what gave him the cred and ability to draw in women that I wanted. I couldn't figure out what separated him so much from a guy like me. Especially where Elizabeth was concerned.

"Have you guys seen Elizabeth around lately?" he asked.

That was odd. Phil and I exchanged a look.

"We were surprised she wasn't in the car with you, man," Phil said.

Tim started laughing. "After last week?" There was an awkward pause, the music on the stereo covering the silence.

"Sorry, Mark," Tim said, very apologetically.

Mark glanced at us through the rearview mirror.

"We kinda had a big fight last week. I think we broke up…"

I tried as hard as I could to play down the intense beams of sunshine and happiness that must have been shooting from my face.

"That sucks, man. We had no idea," Phil said.

"Yeah."

"We're going to go to Chaos right now, if you guys want to ride there with us?"

I could tell Mark wanted a change of subject.

Phil and I hadn't thought we'd make it to the club that night, not after our plans to go downtown for the concert. We counted how much money we had between us.

"Sure!"

As we continued to drive, Tim and Phil talked nonstop about the concert. Mark focused on driving while a million thoughts swam through my head about the news we'd just heard. How did this happen? Why didn't anyone mention it to Phil and me? I also started to actually feel bad for Mark. He did just give us a ride, after all, and if anyone could appreciate what he had just lost I thought it would be me...even though I'd never been in a position to lose it in the first place.

I wondered if he was just trying to be cool by giving us a ride, if it was one person in the scene looking out for another. Or, was he hoping to hear some kind of news about Elizabeth? It could have been some kind of unspoken payback for knocking the guy off him in the pit. Who knew?

When we got inside the club, we found Rachel, Sarah, and Elizabeth hanging out at a table in the corner. They were drunk. When Elizabeth realized we had walked in the door with Mark and his friend, she stormed off toward the bathrooms. Sarah followed her and Rachel slumped drunkenly over the table.

"Who drove?" I asked.

Phil was chasing after Sarah and Elizabeth, and Mark and his friend had already disappeared into to the crowd somewhere.

"I drove," Rachel slurred.

She squinted like she was having trouble finding me.

"We all split a bottle of Bacardi in the parking lot. We used generic cola, which isn't as good as normal Coke, you know? Even with rum."

"Are you going to be able to drive later?"

"Yes, yes, we don't drive drunk. We'll leave at closing. You don't have to get arrested again..." she laughed.

I sat down next to her. I had never seen the girls this sloppy drunk before. It was weird—I had seen Toad that drunk, but not them.

"You know in England they call it drink-driving? How fucked up is that?" she chuckled to herself again and gave me a one-armed hug.

"That rat Mark cheated on Elizabeth, you know? She was upset so we got her drunk!"

It was all coming together, starting to make sense. I guess all the girls having crushes on Mark was too much temptation. He couldn't be faithful, even if it was to the one person that other people would have done anything for.

"You would have been better for her, you know... Oh well, she chose a rat! We caught him in the bathroom last week with some tramp! They were making out!"

Rachel shut herself up as Sarah, Phil, and Elizabeth came back to the table. I could tell from her eyes that Elizabeth had been crying. At that moment I wasn't exactly happy they broke up. I just felt bad for her, for the whole situation. I didn't know what to say.

"Bigmouth Strikes Again" came on just then, like the DJ knew I needed an escape plan.

"I'm gonna go dance," I said. And I headed for the dance floor.

Chapter 12: The Third Sweater Party

My car was now sitting in the garage. It wasn't the most glamorous car, a faded yellow four-door Chevy Citation. It didn't look anything like a hotrod, that's for sure, but it was mine. I was so excited I could finally drive. I made it a point to always keep my board in the trunk. Phil and I vowed to ourselves not to stop skating once we could drive. We knew other skaters who stopped once they could drive. The way we saw it, we could now drive ourselves to new places to skate at.

I had a Cure sticker on the bumper, one that I'd been saving just for this occasion. The car only had a crappy AM stereo so I kept my boombox and some cassettes in the back seat. This greatly increased my battery budget.

Elizabeth had now been broken up with Mark for over a month. I hadn't seen her at the club any more frequently, but I did see Mark every time I went. He was always with a new hot girl.

We were about to get out of school for holiday break and Rob was coming back for the holidays. In honor of his return, Rachel was throwing another Sweater Party. This time Rachel had gone to the trouble of making the flyers herself. She had photocopied a picture of Morrissey and drew a cartoon word bubble to make it look like Morrissey himself was inviting everyone to her house. She was excited to have Rob coming back. Her parents were fighting more and more, and I could tell she was happy to have Rob back for his support.

The Friday before the party, Rachel and Sarah made the rounds at the club and gave invites to people they liked or deemed fit. It had been over a year since the last party and so many of the faces around us had changed. I was curious to see who would show up.

I suffered through a family dinner with my uncle the weekend of the Sweater Party. My entire extended family was conservative, from the south, and made no attempt at hiding their dissatisfaction over my appearance. Whenever they came by for a holiday or something, I had to endure their dirty looks and hushed questions to my parents.

After I escaped from the dinner table, I went and picked up Phil and we drove around in my car and talked about things. We talked about Toad, who had been in a really foul mood at school during the week. We talked about Mark and all the girls we saw him with at the club, and Phil complained about Sarah's parents and their dissatisfaction with him. It seemed like there was always someone deciding something was wrong with us.

After driving around, we broke out our boards and skated a parking lot at a movie theater we found in Arvada. We could get some good speed and ollie up on some parking blocks that were perfect for rail sliding. We were really pulling off some good tricks until we got ran off by someone working for the theater.

"I'll call the cops! I swear the next time you skateboard kids come by, I'm calling the cops!"

We laughed while jumping into my car and throwing our boards into the backseat.

"'Skateboard kids'!" Hilarious.

All in all, it was a pretty good night. When I got home, my uncle was gone.

I helped my mom do some Christmas shopping early the next day. Then I met up with Phil and Toad and headed over to Rachel's to see if we could help prepare for the party.

Toad managed to help her find some liquor that she didn't know was being kept in the house. Toad was always pretty good with that sort of thing; it was one of his natural talents. Now that Rob was gone, their connection to booze was all but gone. So they were encouraging people to bring their own. As we were getting ready to leave, Rob showed up. He had been at the store buying food and snacks. He actually looked a little different. He definitely had gotten more sun than any of us and he looked healthy. He had also gained a little weight. It was strange to me because he hadn't been gone that long. He kept joking it was from all of the beer so readily available in his dorm.

I took Phil home, and then I went to drop off Toad.

"Hey, so, I'm gonna head over to Chaos for a bit, then go to the party," he said, while getting out of my car.

I really didn't want to bring it up but I felt like I had to.

"Okay, cool. Listen, umm… Rachel might get kind of weird if you show up with a bunch of people from the club."

That was the nicest way I could put it. I don't know if he knew what I meant, if he cared, or even if it pissed him off. He nodded and didn't say anything else as he shut the car door. As I drove away, I placed *Uplift Mofo Party Plan* into my boombox. Toad's gruffness wasn't going to get me down. I was in a good mood. The party was tonight, and if Elizabeth showed up it wouldn't be with Mark.

It had seemed so long since the last party. We were already in our second year of high school! I had known these guys for a year now, long enough for Rob to go off to college and to come back for a holiday trip. Long enough to know Elizabeth through two boyfriends. Long enough to finally feel comfortable with everyone, and be *part* of what was going on, instead of *trying* to be part of what was going on. Unfortunately, what was going on that night wasn't much…

Since the obvious scene for Friday nights was now Chaos, the party was unbelievably empty. There were a few people, but for the most part everyone we thought we'd see was at the club. I'd never seen one of Rob and Rachel's parties so empty. It really showed that Rob was the socialite of the two. Rob and Rachel didn't mind that it was empty. I think they were just happy to be together and doing it again.

Phil and Sarah showed up late. At first I thought they had gone to the club like Toad, but it turned out that Sarah's good church-going parents had decided to sit down and grill Phil on his intentions toward their fine daughter. Her father even told Phil that he didn't like his appearance and that he looked like a hoodlum—always wearing that baseball cap. Phil told me that her parents came just short of accusing him of worshipping Satan.

Sarah was really embarrassed about it and went straight to the kitchen for a drink when they arrived. There was tension between the two of them, which was unusual. Phil was stressed, but I was still determined to enjoy the party.

Closer to midnight more people started showing up. I guess they all had the same plan as Toad. Club first, party second. Gabo, Mikey, and

Steve, the clove-smoking deathrockers from the Skinny Puppy show, Tim—they were all slowly arriving.

When Elizabeth showed up, she didn't have her normal glow. She was definitely depressed. Some girls had shown up from the club armed with stories about Mark and some new girl. I'm sure that was exactly what Elizabeth didn't need to hear.

Phil and I were getting really drunk on cheap beer. He found actual generic beer somewhere and had been carrying it around, saving it for another Sweater Party. It was in plain white cans that read BEER in bold black letters. We thought it was hilarious. So he and I kept drinking them and making a show of it in front of anyone we could.

Before we knew it, we were drunk off our asses and the party was filled to somewhat normal capacity.

"I'm telling you what, man. I was on the porch, her parents would barely let me in the house, and then when I got in and they were giving me the third degree, I was so worried they were going to go through my bag or something and find the generic beer. You know how long I've been saving it?"

I was actually surprised when Toad showed up. From his attitude earlier I figured he just wasn't going to make it. He said it took him awhile to get there from the club because he had to walk. I think he was angling for some guilt but I wasn't sure. We invited him in and got him a drink immediately. He was cracking up because he had never seen me drunk before. I was hanging out with him in the kitchen when I noticed something in the other room.

Elizabeth was alone, going through the old *120 Minutes* videos. Without thinking, I walked into the room and sat down next to her. The generic beer was probably helping my confidence or maybe it was just impulsiveness… It could have been either.

"How are you doing?"

She continued watching the TV.

"I'm fine. This isn't the best time for you—"

I interrupted her.

"For me to try to cheer you up?"

I continued, "It's too bad we've never had a chance to really get to know each other. I wish that was different, but it's not. That's fine. I'm fine with that. But, we know each other enough to consider each other friends and that means when I see that you're sad about something I may try to change it. I'm sorry, but that's how I treat my friends."

She cracked a crooked smile, not removing her eyes from the television.

"You can be a pain in the ass, you know that?"

She didn't sound mean. If anything, she might have actually sounded impressed.

"You're a little drunk, huh?"

I shook my head no.

She laughed.

"It's okay. Usually you have your guard up and you worry too much about what everybody thinks."

I think she was still trying to be nice, but those words stung. Maybe because they were true…

"I think it always seems that way around you because I do care what you think." "We barely know each other, why would you care what I think?"

"I don't know. I just always have."

Rachel interrupted us.

"Hey, Rob's making margaritas. Do you guys want one?"

I shook my head no while Elizabeth sprang up from her place on the floor to go get one. It was the same old routine; the moment she had a way out, she took it. I was beginning to get annoyed. I started beating myself up for having tried to cheer her up when she interrupted my thoughts.

"Are you sure you don't want one?" Elizabeth asked from the doorway.

Caught off guard, I shook my head no again.

"Pause the tape for me."

Did that mean she was coming back?

She did indeed come back. She and Rachel came back into the room with huge margaritas. It looked like they filled whatever glasses they could find in the kitchen.

We sat there for a while trying to watch the tape but as the room got more and more crowded with party people, everyone had their own opinion about what video to watch next, so it got annoying. The party had a slow start but had now come to a head. It was crowded, smoky, and kind of frustrating.

I overheard Elizabeth telling Rachel that she wanted to leave as soon as she was sober enough to drive and that all the people were bothering her. I was drunk and I was thinking I couldn't let this moment end yet. We were finally communicating; I had to keep it going. I was feeling buzzed and a little crazed but some how I got an idea.

I told Rachel and Elizabeth to grab their coats and find whoever wanted to get away from the full-blown party. Who knew where Phil and Sarah were off to; I wasn't sure I wanted to find out. I grabbed Toad and some random guy to help me out.

We grabbed every cushion from every couch in the house and as many blankets as we could find from the linen closet. The people at the party didn't even notice what we were doing, and the few who did just thought we were crazy. Luckily, Rachel was buzzed enough to find what we were doing funny.

In a small group not unlike the one at the first Sweater Party, we all stealthily scaled the fence and walked out into the black space of the Vita-Course. The only difference was that this time we were armed with blankets and cushions.

It took awhile to walk to the middle of the soccer fields because Rachel and Elizabeth were laughing so hard at us. Toad and I could barely walk with all the cushions and blankets.

"If you think you're gonna to get lucky out here, let me tell you, you're out of luck, mister!" Rachel said, laughing.

"We're building a fort," I said. "Just like the kind you'd make when you were a kid."

"I totally used to build forts!"

"A couch cushion fort?"

"I never did that."

"Now's your chance."

They couldn't stop laughing at my idea. I guess I was pretty buzzed. But soon they were arguing over the best way to stand up the cushions and hang blankets over them. Even the brooding Toad lightened up, talking about how he'd pretend his cushion forts were submarines when he was a kid. The random guy who came out with us began talking about how he'd pretend he was in the *Millennium Falcon* in his cushion fort. He even went back a couple of times to get some lawn furniture to help our construction.

A short while later the couch cushion fort had been erected. We were inside talking and sharing stories. It was dark, but felt warm. Elizabeth didn't quite glow the way she used to, but at least she looked happier than she had a couple hours before.

Rachel had brought a bottle of vodka. She kept sipping from it, making a funny face and speaking.

"If my parents come home and find grass stains on the couch, first they are gonna wonder what the hell happened, then they're gonna kill me! And if they kill me I'll have to kill you!"

Toad snickered to himself, then took a drink off the vodka bottle which Rachel had just passed him.

When I closed my eyes, my head would spin. I wasn't sure if it was the mood or the liquor...probably the liquor. Our fort looked pretty damn cool—our proud creation standing in the stark black of the empty field. As it got colder, some of the others left, including Rachel and Elizabeth. Elizabeth made it a point to say goodbye to me, and Rachel made it a point to tell us she'd kill us if we forgot to bring any of the cushions back to the house.

As I watched them disappear, I replayed Elizabeth saying goodnight to me in my head. That was enough to make me happy. That's what I needed, some recognition, a positive interaction. I finally had that.

We were very proud of our creation and I didn't realize how cold it was as Toad and I fell asleep in our couch cushion fort.

Daylight.

"Excuse me?"

It sounded like an older man.

"Excuse me?"

I slowly knocked down one of the cushion-walls. As it fell, I saw a man dressed as a referee and what looked like an entire team of peewee soccer players gathered around peering at us. The kids were all confused and their parents pissed-off.

It was morning, half of our cushion fort was knocked down and some sort of soccer championship waiting to get underway on the field. Toad stirred from underneath his blanket. The tuft of green on top of his head flopped as he rubbed his eyes, looking around.

"You need to get out of here or I'll call the police!"

The man was dressed in the authority of a referee outfit. Toad and I nodded our heads like we knew what he was saying and tiredly woke up our new friend. I still didn't know his name. The three of us started moving the pieces of the fort back toward Rachel's house.

As we got closer to the house I could see Rachel hurriedly walking across the field toward us. She was in fresh clothes for the new day and looked really upset about something. She had tears in her eyes.

"Phil called. He's been trying to get a hold of you. They're looking for you. Something's wrong with your dad. You're supposed to go to the hospital right now!"

She bit her lip.

"They think it was a heart attack…"

Everything around me froze for a moment. No sound, no wind, no temperature. Everything blank.

In that spot. In that moment. Things changed.

I got back to Rachel's house on some kind of numb autopilot. I got into my car.

"Please, let us drive you to the hospital," Rachel pleaded.

"Yeah, you don't look good. You're really pale."

Rob and Rachel looked so concerned.

"I'll be fine. I just need to go."

With that, I took off down the street. The truth was I didn't want them to see me crying as I drove. I was scared. I probably broke every traffic and speeding law on the books. The whole time I was driving, at every damn red light I got stopped at, I would fear that my dad would die and I wouldn't be there for him. I was already so pissed at myself. I couldn't believe something happened to him and I was out nowhere to be found having *fun* with my friends.

I pulled up to the hospital and found some crappy parking spot and ran inside. I was so agitated I couldn't figure out where he was. The woman behind the desk didn't know what to say or do. She had no idea who I was there for. Finally I saw my next-door-neighbor emerge from a double door. The door had a cold sort of sheet metal on it and closed slowly behind him.

He walked over to me and before he said anything he just gave me a hug. It was odd. It felt very odd. It confirmed that something horrible was really happening.

"Where's my mom and dad?"

My neighbor still had his hand on my shoulder.

"Where are they?" I demanded.

"Let's sit down for a second. I want you to know everything that's going on before you go in there."

I wanted to go immediately. But it felt like I didn't have a choice.

"Early this morning, your father woke up with chest pains. They thought he was having a heart attack and called the ambulance. Right before it got to the house, he collapsed and they had to try to revive him. They got his heart started again but he has been unconscious since it happened. Right now your mom's in there with him and he's on some devices that are monitoring him. They are trying to come up with the best plan so they can help him."

I didn't say anything. It was hitting me hard. A deafening silence was filling my ears and my chest. My neighbor squeezed my shoulder and looked me in the eye.

"Let's go in," he said. "And you be strong for your mother."

We walked through the double doors and into a place that had walls made of curtains. My mom looked over at me from where she was sitting. I could tell she had just been looking over my father. I could also see she had been crying. I had never seen my mother cry.

My neighbor left the room behind me as my gaze fell on my dad. He was laying there, his eyes closed and he looked like he was asleep. There were tubes going into his mouth and nose. I remember thinking that the tubes going down his throat would hurt later when he came out of it.

My mom brokenly got out of her chair and gave me a hug. I didn't know what to say. I didn't know what to do. I just stood there.

"I'm sorry I wasn't home."

I really was.

"It's okay. You got here as soon as you could."

We sat down. We just sat for a while and watched him. Every now and then he would stir and I would hope he was waking up. I will never forget the haunting sound of those machines and their mechanical beeps for the rest of my life. I'll never forget the sterile smell of the place. I hated that place.

A doctor with an accent and a clipboard came in and discussed something quietly with my mom. I watched as he pointed things out on diagrams and monitors.

Then the uncle who didn't like me much showed up. Not that he was a total bad guy—he did try to ask me how I was doing. After we talked for a minute he walked my mom down to the vending machines to get her a cup of coffee.

I was left alone with my father.

I just sat there, looking at the face of the man who I'd called father my whole life. He was silent. He looked like he needed a shave. I kept trying to talk to God inside my head and ask him to wake up my dad while I was sitting there. Since we were alone, I tried to talk to him. It was hard with the lump in my throat. I wasn't sure if he was listening or if he could even hear me but I told him that I loved him. I told him I would be good to my mother and that I'd work hard, like he had to work hard when he was a kid.

He died three days later.

Chapter 13: Small Glittering Lights

My mom and I walked around numb and lifeless during the days that followed. We were pale ghosts; we didn't eat, didn't sleep; we didn't really exist. Those days of being alive had been taken from us, along with my father.

My uncle moved in temporarily so someone would be with my mom and could help take care of all the things that had to be taken care of. There's more to deal with when somebody dies than you would ever think to care about or deal with. I wanted to help, I really did, but I was crippled with the numbness. A fog of depression clung to me, rendering me useless.

I missed school the rest of the week. While my mother was out one day, I found myself home alone. I just kept walking around the house looking around. I wasn't looking for anything in particular. But my mind was wandering and I couldn't stop moving. Since I was the only one home, I used their stereo. I played the music really loud. I must have gone through every tape I owned over and over. I'd listen to certain songs, trying to console myself, trying to heal myself with the music. The sounds, the lyrics—it was a distraction, a medicine I was trying to use.

I was startled out of my musical healing by a knock on the door. It was Mr. Dorris, my school counselor. He was with a woman who was supposed to be some type of grief counselor. It was weird having a faculty member from my school in my house. It felt queer and I didn't care for the collision of worlds. I didn't care for any of it.

They sat in my living room for a while and tried to "talk" to me. Every now and then they would exchange serious looks. I just tried to keep my cool so they would leave. As soon as I could, I said goodbye to them. They assured me not to worry about my grades or classes and that my teachers would be understanding. They also asked me to get some rest.

Mr. Dorris looked just as nervous and frail as the first time I had met him. I seemed to be handling things better than he was. Or at least that's what I thought. Waves of grief were crashing over me. I'd tell myself I was okay, I would tell myself I would be strong and pull through, I would get through this for my mother. Then a moment later I was fucking crazy again. Mad at the world and right back where I started from, helpless. It was an emotional roller coaster. I was being held underwater, not allowed to come up for air.

I had kept my cool while they were there. I hadn't lost my shit. I showed a good face and I was charming and strong. As soon as they were gone, I went back to pacing through the house.

Then I made a discovery that made me come unglued. A box of drywall screws... My father and I had bought them a couple weeks prior for work on the half-pipe. I looked at the unopened box of screws in my hand and thought about the skeleton of the half-pipe in the backyard.

I walked out back with the box clutched in hand and I stared at the unfinished structure. It stood like a tombstone. Pointless posts coming from the ground leading to a structure that would never go anywhere or become anything.

He was really gone.

Crying. Pleading. I tossed the box of screws across the backyard. It exploded in a shower of metal as it hit the fence.

In front of others, I kept my cool. I kept it all in. I didn't want anyone to see me crying. I didn't want to let my guard down. My neighbor's words whirled through my head: "Be strong for your mother."

Phil's family sent flowers to my house. The flowers sat in the front room with countless other arrangements of flowers from people I didn't know.

There was an arrangement from Rachel and Rob's family as well. But the most helpful person was probably Toad's mom. I never even saw her that much and she had never met my mom before, but she stopped by one day with Toad's ornery little siblings in tow and brought us a huge dinner she had cooked that could be re-heated if needed.

I wondered if she had done that because they couldn't afford to do things like buy flowers. But it was far more useful than flowers. We still needed to eat. We needed to take care of ourselves, but in the death-fog we had forgotten how. My mom, uncle, and I finished every last bit of that food. It was needed at a time when we didn't even have the strength to cook a meal for ourselves.

Toad didn't know how to act.

"My old man's a scumbag, fucking disappeared when I was a kid. Pisses me off someone cool like your dad died. Should've been someone like my dad."

It was sad, but there was logic to it. I had a father who was good but died; he had a father who was lousy but was still out there somewhere ignoring his mom and his family. For different reasons, Toad and I both were fucked. I don't know what exactly he was going through, but he seemed to be in just as bad a place as me.

To my surprise, I got a call from Elizabeth. She must have gotten my number from Rachel.

"I hope you're doing okay. If you need anything you can call me."

They were comforting words, even in the state I was in. She also said that she had appreciated when I was trying to cheer her up at the party and that she thought I was a good person. It wasn't the brooding Elizabeth that I'd known from art class the year before. That year seemed so far away now. Those days seemed so far behind me... They were innocent compared to now. They didn't hurt in the same way as now.

It was December. Everyone in the world was getting ready for a happy Christmas with his or her family. Everyone except for my mom and me. We were preparing to drive down south for a funeral. I always hated having to go to my father's hometown, and I knew this trip would be the worst.

The day before we were to leave, I got another call from Elizabeth. Rachel had told her I'd be leaving for the funeral and she was wondering if I wanted to go get coffee the night before to get my mind off things.

I couldn't believe it. It was strange. I hung up the phone feeling guilty. I felt like such an asshole for letting my mom see me happy.

"What was that all about?" she asked.

The guilt continued as I explained it to her. I told her about Elizabeth and some of the things that had gone on between us the last year and that she was offering to take me out to get coffee. My mom patted my arm and spoke.

"It's okay to be happy about something. It might be all we have to get through this, and that's okay. It's okay to be happy about something. You don't feel bad about it, okay?"

At that moment, I was so glad my mom was my mom. Relieved from the weight that was momentarily suffocating me, we talked for a while longer, and then she went to speak with my uncle about the drive we'd make tomorrow. Instead of dreading that drive I thought about the night in front of me. Hopefully tonight would last forever and I would never have to find myself in tomorrow.

I picked up Elizabeth at her sister's place. I guess she had been living with her sister for almost a year. She didn't care to explain how she ended up there and I figured I shouldn't ask.

Elizabeth came running from the front door in her long winter coat and climbed into my car. Her angelic face wore the glow she'd had the night of the first Sweater Party. A snowflake would fall down every now and then but it wasn't really snowing. It was a cold night, the kind where the night air stings your face.

We went to Perkin's for coffee and sat talking. We talked about all kinds of things, except for where I would be going the next day. We talked about different bands, people we knew, Phil and Sarah's relationship, everything. We ordered pie and had more coffee. As she handed the menu back to the waitress I made it a point to remember that she liked pumpkin pie. I filed it away in the back of my mind along with her love of Martin Gore, and the videos she had selected off Rachel's *120 Minutes* list.

A couple people we knew from Chaos came in and sat in a booth near us. I felt a flash of pride when they came in and saw me sitting with Elizabeth. It was strange sitting there with her. In some ways, I felt like I had never really looked her in the face until then. We had never really made eye contact before. I guess the state of shock I was in helped.

We got bored of Perkin's and decided to drive around. We drove around different neighborhoods, every so often passing a twinkling house bearing Christmas lights. There were stories hidden in those lights, stories hidden in the dark that surrounded them. They passed us by like blessings or maybe like ghosts. The small glittering lights on each house told stories of the lives that went on inside.

I had the album *Disintegration* in my boombox in the backseat. I had been listening to it a lot lately. With the cold outside, her next to me, and the music playing, I felt like I was going to crumble to pieces inside. Not from sadness but from the beauty of the moment. She was so beautiful in the near dark. And for that moment we were warm. I knew that it wouldn't last. I knew that the next day everything would be different. But at least I had this moment.

We got back to her place and I didn't want to drop her off; I didn't want it to end. We sat there for a long time without saying a word. I wore a pained expression on my face and she looked at me with the same intense stare from art class. It was like she was trying to figure out a puzzle.

In the dark car, only part of her face was lit from the porch light and now that we were stopped the cold was biting in from the car windows.

"You know, at that party, when you jumped on that Brad guy because of Rachel, I thought that was really good of you. And before, when you wouldn't let Sarah drive home drunk and you got in all of that trouble… I thought that was really good of you, too. And I appreciate you sticking up for Mark at the club that night."

She laughed a little.

"He's a jerk, but I saw you and Toad try to help him that night."

I didn't know what to say. I just took a good, long look at her.

Then she spoke again.

"Back at the parties and in that art class you seemed so happy and innocent… You have to try not to lose that, okay?"

She leaned forward and gave me a hug. I held onto her for as long as I could. I could smell her hair and feel her breathing.

"Goodnight. We'll all be thinking about you."

Then she headed off hurriedly into the house, still bundled in her winter coat. As I sat there in my car, she turned and waved, then closed the door behind her.

Where did the time go?

I drove homeward. In an uneasy way, I was at least feeling happy about the evening. With my mother's words still hanging in my ear, I tried to simply enjoy what had just happened. I thought about Elizabeth intensely. I thought about her trying to take my mind off things. I wanted to thank her somehow.

I stopped at a grocery store that was open 24 hours. It was as vacant as I was feeling. I found the floral department, if you could call it that, and picked out a rose. I decided I would take it to her place and leave it on her doorstep or something. I would figure that part out when I got there.

The old lady at the checkout kept peering at me through her horn-rimmed glasses and kept trying to figure out what I was up to. I couldn't tell if she thought I was being sweet or creepy. I guess it's a fine line.

"Those flowers for your girlfriend?"

A man behind me in line chuckled.

"This time of night, you buying flowers? You must be in the doghouse."

"No, it's just for a friend," I said.

Both the checkout lady and the man behind me seemed disappointed. I think she wanted to believe in some larger-than-life romance and he wanted to hear some kind of drama. I thought it best to get going. In just hours I was going to climb into the car with my mom and my uncle to drive to my father's funeral.

I parked a couple houses down and walked up to her doorstep. It was cold and silent once I turned my car off. The best place to leave the flower was indeed the doorstep. I crept up, wondering if that was how burglary felt and I carefully set the rose on the doormat.

Driving home, I noticed all of the traffic lights were flashing yellow. It reminded me of the night Phil and I drove around together talking about life. When I got home and to bed, thoughts of Elizabeth swam around in my head. But they weren't alone. The fear of the funeral was a dark cloud that hovered near. I was scared.

When I got up the next morning, it was cold and grey. I felt terrible, like I hadn't even slept. I decided I should go out and brush the snow off the car and warm it up for my mom. Pulling my coat collar up, I stepped out onto the front porch and found something lying in front of me. Sitting on our doormat was a single rose.

We drove for a day and a half. The skies were gray and stormy the entire way. The trees on the side of the road were dead and leafless for winter. The lonely emptiness of the two-lane highway couldn't have been more symbolic.

As we made our way across the barren wasteland, I kept secretly removing the rose from my bag. Careful not to be seen with it, I'd study it, distracting myself with thoughts of how it got to my doorstep and what it meant. It was one of the few comforts I had out there on that road.

We would pass state lines, small towns, and countless strangers on the road. I kept wondering about their stories, wondering if they had ever felt as bad as I did now, if they had any idea what a sad convoy we really were.

The funeral was set on a hilltop. Rolling hills adorned with the markers of death stretched all around us. It was a brisk morning, but at least the sun had come out.

I had spent the last twenty-four hours being hugged, squeezed, and often judged by people who I didn't know but that my mom assured me were family or family friends. Some would talk to me about my father when he was young, some would compare my looks to his, and others would look disapprovingly at me.

Getting the dirty looks from *family members* sucked. Their small-town reactions made me angry; they made me want to find more ways to offend them. Who did they think they were? This wasn't the time for them to judge me. No matter what they were thinking, they should have kept it to themselves. They should have made an attempt to be decent. *Their* father didn't just die right there in front of them. *They* hadn't had to watch their mom crying for the last week. Who did they think they were!

The funeral home was a family business, and it being a small town, everyone pretty much knew everyone else. Except for my mom and me. I was angry that I was sitting there feeling like a stranger at my own father's funeral. These people didn't know what my mother and I had just been through—at the hospital, in the days that followed, on the road. They didn't know who my father was when he died. How could they know the man that I knew?

I was sick the entire day of the funeral. I guess it was nerves more than anything else. I was so weak and run-down I worried I wouldn't have the strength to be a pallbearer. I had never been a pallbearer before and I was nervous about it, but I knew it was something I had to do. I didn't want to regret not having done it.

The physical weight of the casket matched the mental burden I was carrying. As I held on to the brass railing, I knew I would never forget this for the rest of my life. The permanence of the moment would never leave me.

Different people stood up and said nice things about my father. Then a small town Johnny Cash of a man sang "Amazing Grace" on a six-string guitar. As he played, and people wept I looked out across the hills in the distance. The singer played on, his blonde pompadour rustled in the wind as he strummed away. People I didn't know were crying, my mother was sobbing, and I couldn't help thinking how cool that guy with the guitar was. I was glad he was there. It made me feel better. I pondered what his story was, and it helped take away some of the pain from the moment.

Somehow we survived the day. We made it. We just had to spend one more night in the damn hick town and in the morning we could escape. After the funeral, we were taken to my great aunt's house, where people gathered. They ate, consoled one another and had conversations.

"It was a nice service."

"It was a lovely day for a service."

"Such a shame, he was still a young man."

"Is that how the kids in the city are fixing their hair?"

"He was the nicest man."

"Is that an earring?"

"Everyone loved your father, son."

"Want some more fried chicken?"

"Such a shame."

"Here, you need to eat."

"Yeah, we're gonna miss him..."

On the drive back home, my mom was in pretty bad condition. Her nerves finally caught up with her and she was sick. My uncle was tired from driving and they were trying to decide if we should stop in some small town for a motel. All I wanted to do was go home and never think about any of this ever again.

"I can drive for a while," I said sheepishly.

My mother was hesitant at first, because I hadn't had my license for that long. Luckily, she was so anxious to get home that she agreed. I drove for hours through the great open space. The skies were still grey and the trees were still dead. Patches of dirty snow were gathered in clumps on the side of the road. When I was sure both my mom and my uncle were asleep I would drive fast and when they awoke I would drive normal. I just wanted to get home. Toward the end of the journey my mom awoke, giving me a funny look.

"You've driven almost the entire way?" she said.

I nodded.

"Your father would have been proud of you."

With those words in my head, we continued homeward.

Chapter 14: Return of the Combat Boots

T he strangest thing happened the day I went back to school. In one of my classes the teacher and the entire class bought a grievance card and went through the trouble of signing it. The thing that annoyed me about it was that *everyone* signed it, including people who I didn't know and people who used to hate me. When I saw that guy Tom had signed it, I thought to myself, last year he's throwing my skateboard in that goddamn sewer, and now he's writing me a message saying that he hopes everything works out. How fucking inconsistent. Make a choice, man, and stick with it! I had only been back a day and I was already tired of hearing people say, "I'm so sorry," or "I'm sorry, man," especially if they didn't know me. What the hell did they know?

After that odd experience, Phil and I left the school for lunch. I didn't feel like explaining everything over and over at the Freak Table. Phil caught me up on everything I had missed while I was away at the funeral.

"Man, you could've skipped out on more school, I bet," Phil said while squirting hot sauce into his mouth. His food was already in there waiting for it, a very charming skill of his.

"Yeah, well, I was ready to get out of the house," I told him. "Besides, I really missed these bastards."

We agreed to go out to the club and get absolutely fucking drunk that night. I was ready for it. The past couple of weeks had been an eternity and I wanted to get back to some kind of normal. We talked about Elizabeth and I told him about the evening before the funeral. I told him about everything that happened, except for the rose. For some reason, I didn't want to tell anyone about that. I wanted that memory to be all mine.

After some hesitation, Phil asked about the funeral. I didn't mind. He had never been to a funeral and was just as uncomfortable about it as I was. He listened intently as I told him about the guitar singer, how I was relieved when I found out it was closed casket, and about all the annoying relatives who kept making comments about the way I looked.

Toad was nowhere to be found after lunch. His yearly tradition was to skip the last day of school before Christmas vacation; it was a Christmas miracle he even made it for the first half of the day.

As night fell, I had the house to myself—I seemed to have it to myself a lot lately. My mom was always at friends' or somewhere where people were trying to feed her or cheer her up. As I was getting ready to go to the club, I went out into the garage and found an old bottle of Cutty Sark. It must have been sitting in the cabinet for at least ten years. I did a shot of it followed by some Coke we had in the fridge. Man, was it fierce. I almost wondered if they kept it out in the garage to take paint off brushes or something.

I was playing "So What" by Ministry. I could feel anger percolating through my blood; I didn't know if it was the music or the shot of whiskey. I kept looking at myself in the mirror and thinking about how the person looking back was alone. That was a contrast to even a month before when it would have been Toad, Phil, and I crammed in front of that mirror all trying to make ourselves look *cool*.

I thought about Elizabeth again and about the night before the funeral. I already felt like that night was ages ago.

I placed the whiskey in the trunk of my car. As I was locking up the house, I remembered the combat boots up in my closet. I looked down at my feet and the sneakers on them. The boots fit my mood. They fit the anger. I ran back into my room, laced up the boots, and tucked my pants in. One part of my life dissolved away while an angrier one was born.

It was freezing outside, cold but not cloudy. The sky was black, no clouds to hold in the heat. As I walked out to my car I felt like I was looking up from the surface of the moon.

I pulled up to Phil's house with a skid, popped a piece of cinnamon gum in my mouth and waited. Once he was in the car we were off. I wanted a crazy night and somewhere in my young blood the whiskey was prickling.

We parked and sat by an old warehouse near the strip mall where the club was located. In front of us was a field of castaways: pieces of old cars, refrigerators, and anything else people didn't want to bother taking to the dump. It was somewhat of a junk graveyard. We passed the bottle back and forth, taking shots while throwing rocks at some sort of appliance in the distance. Every now and then we'd hit it, causing a loud metal *ding* followed by our drunken giggles. We were completely loaded.

"This isn't gonna beat me, man. It's not gonna affect me, you know. I'm gonna beat these odds and go on and do well in life, ya know? I'm sad, but I'll get through."

"Yeah, you will, man. I know you will. You ever hear about Elvis? He didn't have a dad real young, and look at him. He became all rich and famous and took good care of his mom."

Phil took another swig from the bottle and I looked around at the field in front of us, contemplating if the world we lived in even had any need for more Elvises.

My mood was up and down and all over the place. When the whiskey was gone we fought over who would throw the empty bottle. Phil conceded and let me throw it. I'm sure it was pity on his part. I tossed it as hard as I could. When it crashed and broke it was like this fucked-up music to our ears. We howled, pleased with its destruction.

The minute we got inside the club I could hear Ministry playing. Rachel and Sarah tried to say hello but I brushed passed them, almost running toward the pit. I felt like I needed it.

I didn't look around, I didn't think, I just followed my anger. People were flying around, the strobe lights were flashing, the movement was once again surrounding me. Hands grabbed at me, tearing, pulling, and pushing. My arms were flailing around and my hands were in fists. I came around the circle and saw Toad coming around the opposite way. His eyes were crazed; my eyes were crazed. We had tapped into the anger the world had been offering us. I finally understood. I understood why this had to exist.

Toad grabbed me and threw me into the wall of people. I knocked some guy hard; he pushed me back into Toad. I kept laughing. The anger was surging through me. I stomped around, taking exaggerated steps while I pushed, punched, and threw. The strobes flashed white. Every now and then a leather jacket, blue hair, or bald head would fly by. Every now and then I would get knocked down or knock someone down. It didn't matter.

After the song ended, Toad and I stood there catching our breaths. I felt great. I felt the running of my blood. Rachel, Sarah, and Phil came over to us. Rachel scolded me for brushing past them.

"I really needed to get in the pit and let loose. Sorry, feeling better now."

Then, I realized how much better I wasn't feeling. I was thirsty, really thirsty. And something was wrong in my chest. It was hard to breathe or to focus.

"I'm going to the bar to get some water."

As I stumbled away, I thought I heard Sarah yelling at Phil for us being so drunk. I didn't care. I needed a night like this. They should understand that. As I tried to fill a small plastic cup with water, I felt a tap on my shoulder. I turned to find one of the big skinheads that Toad had been hanging out with.

"Little Toad told me about your pop, sorry to hear it."

He reached out his hand to shake. I never pictured myself shaking the hand of a skinhead. I was drunk, so I reached out and shook his hand. He squeezed firmly as he shook, then patted me on the shoulder.

"Anyone fucks with you, we'll take care of 'em. I know what it's like, kid."

I just nodded. I was so drunk and confused. I didn't know what to say back to him. It was the first time one of those guys seemed human. A couple of his friends walked up and were laughing at how drunk I was. I excused myself, stumbling away. I was getting uncomfortable, feeling sick.

As I walked away, the brooding look of concern on that skinhead's face was burned into my vision. I couldn't get the look out of my head. I stumbled past a group of people and was stopped by Steve, Mikey, and Gabo. Mikey and Gabo got in my face.

"What the fuck are you doing?"

They motioned to where I had just come from. I turned around and looked, then turned back to them.

"I'm fucking drunk, man."

They cracked up laughing.

"You should be careful. You're too young to be that fucking drunk, dude."

"Why the fuck you hanging out with those guys?"

I swayed a bit. Steve and Gabo instantly recognized the look on my face.

Steve walked me to the bathroom as quickly as he could. When we got inside, it was packed; no stalls were open. Panicked, I looked around through my drunken haze. I was gonna puke hard. Steve cleared a path to one of the sinks. He then held me up while I puked my guts out all over the mirror and sink.

The next thing I remember was sitting on the curb eating some bread someone had given me. Next to me was a pile of bread crusts that I must have been pulling off. A few feet away from me on the other side was more puke. Gabo was chuckling to himself as he, Steve, and Phil leaned against a car looking down at me.

"You're gonna fill that gutter up and we'll have to move even further down the block, dude," said Gabo, his mohawk backlit from the streetlight behind him. Steve and Phil were drinking coffee from paper cups. Steve spoke.

"You kept puking in the sink and then this drag queen came over doing this Florence Nightingale shit trying to take care of you. You kept puking and everybody in there was either laughing their ass off or running for cover. Finally security came in and said we had to leave *immediately.*"

Gabo interrupted, "You told the bouncers kicking you out to go and blow each other!"

They all started laughing.

"He did not!" Phil spoke up, still laughing.

I rubbed my aching temples.

"Then what happened?"

"The bouncers were really pissed off and gave us this speech how you were banned for life, and all this shit!"

Phil cut in.

"That's when I saved your ass and told them you had a shitty week and I'd get you out of there."

Phil must have opted to look after me instead of going home with Sarah like they'd planned… These guys were all right. I was sick, and my mind was cloudy, but I kept thinking how good these guys were to me. Deciding to leave my car, Phil and I got a ride home from Steve and Gabo. As Gabo drove, Phil and Steve kept talking. Phil asked Steve why he didn't drive. He was college age after all.

"I was really drunk one night and I kind of wrecked a car. I didn't get caught by the cops or anything but the cost of the insurance killed us. To make it worse, my mom had an accident within the same six months and the rate really shot up. So I don't drive. I walk."

When we got to my house, we tried to get inside as quietly as possible. I didn't want to wake my mom in the condition I was in, nor did I want to explain how we'd gotten home. I was too sick to fall asleep; instead, I lay down with my cheek flush to the floor. I looked across the ground, which was now hung at a cruel angle. As I waited to pass out, I felt like a defeated villain in an old episode of *Batman*.

The next morning I was painfully hung over.

The next few months would go very much in the same manner. It was the coldest part of the year in more ways than one. I wore the boots every day; spikes were placed in some of the eyelets and the sneakers stayed in the closet along with my skateboard. My hair was now black and completely out of control. It was shaved around the sides and the rest stuck up in a fin of spikes.

Unfortunately, I wasn't the only one changing. During the two-week Christmas break, Toad went through a transformation of his own. His mom must have bought him a burgundy flight jacket for Christmas. That alone wouldn't mean much. But when he came to school the first day after break he looked completely different. His signature green sprout of hair was gone, his head now completely shaved. He wore red laces in his boots, braces, and the flight jacket. There was no more speculation. He was heading down a different path than the rest of us, a dark path. The clouds we had all seen on the horizon of the scene had come for him.

We all saw it coming, but didn't think it would go this far. He looked angry. We all looked angry, but his face had changed. He was different and none of us agreed with it. The day he showed up to school looking that way was a test for all of us. Who was still going to be cool to him? Who was going to avoid him? Who was going to do something about it?

Also, there was the question of who was going to end up jumping him. It was just a matter of time. Standing up for Toad because he was different was one thing. Standing up for Toad because he had a big mouth was another, both of which I could deal with. But his new look—and what it suggested—I couldn't stand up for him for that. If it came down to it, he would be on his own now. Maybe an ass-kicking is what he'd need to snap him out of it? None of us knew.

Neither Toad nor I were skating anymore but for completely different reasons. I just wasn't feeling it lately. Skating had become something you were into when you were younger. And I wasn't feeling so young. I didn't have the luxury of a young person's concerns. All of a sudden I had much bigger things to worry about.

Exactly what I was doing instead of skating, I don't know. Hanging out at people's houses, getting coffee at Perkin's, going to the club. Not really doing anything, just hanging out. I couldn't hang out with Phil and Toad at the same time anymore. When Toad showed up to school looking like a skin, Phil got pissed and refused to hang out with or be seen with him.

Toad swore up and down that he wasn't like the other guys he was hanging with. I figured he would eventually snap out of it. Times were fucked up, not just for me, but for everyone. The scene was changing. More and more people were coming around, people from our school, from other schools. It was getting crowded and factions and groups were forming.

Rachel and Sarah didn't care for Toad's new look, either. Rachel was furious with him. At least she convinced him to switch back to black laces. Maybe I would have tried harder or maybe I would have cared more, but I busy was dealing with my own problems.

The only thing I was doing with consistency was getting drunk and hanging out. That was probably why Toad and I were still able to talk to each other; he was doing much of the same.

Elizabeth had all but disappeared again. I didn't see or hear from her after I got back from the funeral. I thought I would see her, I hoped I would, but it just didn't happen. Maybe she was just being nice that night? Maybe it was pity?

One afternoon after lunch at school, Sarah gave me a slight report.

"Elizabeth told me to tell you hi for her."

"Has she been around?"

"No, not really. Nobody's really seen her. I'm starting to think more shit is going on with her family. She really hasn't been around at all."

At first I thought Elizabeth was avoiding me because of the exchange we had the night before the funeral. It seemed too good to be true…more friendly and intimate than Elizabeth was comfortable with, maybe?

I didn't know what to think of her, but I decided to forget it. Elizabeth was off dealing with whatever it was she had to deal with and I was dealing with what I had to. I had other things to worry about besides her. Life had kicked me hard in the side and I was responding. My anger was growing and I didn't see it as a problem; it was a fuel, and these people just didn't understand. They had guarantees in life; they had Kodak Moments. I had to survive.

My grades were slipping. I didn't care. I had to get a job, so I was focused on that. The life insurance from my father went to paying off the mortgage, and that was all. That left both my mom and I living on her small income so I figured for the things I wanted or needed I better start making some money. If the people at school giving the grades couldn't understand that then fuck 'em. I jumped right into the American dream and got a job that sucked big and paid little.

Besides bad grades at school and working part-time, there was also another new problem I had to deal with. Not in the streets, clubs, or in school, a problem in my very home, the one place that should have been safe ground. This guy wasted no time moving in on my mom. He was a *friend* of my father's from work. I kind of remembered seeing him around sometimes at the building sites but I really didn't think of him as someone *close* to my family.

He had been around *consoling* and *looking out* for my mom. Before I knew it, he and my mother were dating. Before I knew it, he was around the house all the time. He couldn't stand me or my friends or the way we looked. He did his best to disguise it from my mom, but I knew. And when she wasn't around he didn't bother with the nice guy act.

I heard him more than once discussing my friends and me with my mother when he didn't think I was around. He'd go off on rants about what *he* thought we were. He couldn't have been more prejudiced or more far away from the truth. He was a hick and didn't understand my friends or what we were about.

But that wasn't the worst of it. What was getting to me more than anything was that he was suddenly a barrier between my mother and me. He was just accepted as part of our lives and suddenly I was the one having to defend myself to him and his ideas of what was normal. I guess she was happy and I knew that was important, but now I was a stranger in my own house. It was like I'd lost both parents and was left to fend for myself.

My friends helped, the scene helped, even the music helped. The stark melancholy and desolate feelings ran through all of us. I wasn't alone. At least we all had the scene. At least we had that in common. Maybe it was for different reasons, but we were all together on that edge.

One cold night, I climbed into my car and drove really far out. I wasn't going anywhere in particular. I just drove. I ended up at the edge of town near some new neighborhoods that were being built. It looked like it would be wealthy area. I parked my car out there, with the rich people's yards behind me and a dark nothingness in front of me. No streetlights, no civilization, just an open field with a patch of frozen snow in the distance.

I sat there by myself playing Sisters of Mercy on my boombox. The car was shut off. The cold was just outside the windows, waiting for me. I was freezing…and I was listening. Really listening.

I now truly understood the desperation of all of us who had changed ourselves. I understood those who didn't fit in and those who were hurting. We marked ourselves so others on the battlefield could see us. I don't know if it worked. I don't know if we were ever really seen for what we were. Wounded.

Chapter 15: He's Lost Control

It was already spring. I could hardly believe that before I knew it, the school year would be over. So much was happening personally, I'd lost track of the changes happening on a larger scale. I was so caught up with my own problems that the larger, broader changes snuck up on me and the other members of the Freak Table... Something happened that none of us could have prepared for...

The Buzz Clip

Smells Like Teen Spirit

Nirvana

Grunge

The Downward Spiral

Alternative

In the course of one school year, everything changed. After years of ridicule, years of having to stand up for myself, suddenly all that I held dear had become a gimmick. By the end of the school year, we started to see people from our fucking school appearing at the clubs we went to, the very places that were our refuges because we weren't welcome anywhere else. Now these fuckers were following us into our hiding places. I was so pissed about it. I was pissed about a lot of things, but this was the icing on the pissed-off-cake.

One night at Chaos, Phil and I were hanging out playing pool. "Motorbike" by Sheep On Drugs was playing and everything was great until a preppy girl from school came over to us. I was waiting for Phil to make a shot when she walked up. She was nervous, trying to make conversation and blend in. She stood close and watched us play for a while until she timidly spoke.

"I remember when those guys used to mess with you in history class," she said to me. "They were such assholes. I couldn't understand why they were always so mean to you. I was always so mad at them for that."

Then why didn't you say anything? I thought. I really didn't care to give her a response at all.

"Yeah, well, people are assholes…" I said, then turned my back to her and continued my game of pool.

Everywhere we went was getting overrun and everything we were was suddenly a way for someone else to sell a product. They took it. They exploited it. They sold us out, and they ruined us. The messages that our music and our lifestyle was trying to get across was now lost somewhere in their acceptance.

I didn't care how many of them started piercing things, dyeing things, wearing and buying things—they didn't understand what had brought us here and away from them in the first place. With the creation of Alternative, a culture wasn't born; instead, another culture was killed.

It was bad enough losing my dad. It was bad enough that my mom and I were now so distant. But now my friends and I were losing our identities to the *mainstream*. They came in with their approval and were taking as much from us as they could in return. If all of this wasn't bad enough, the once-united members of the Freak Table were splintering apart.

I was the only one who would still hang around with Toad. Not if he was with his *other* friends, but if it was just him and I. One day we even tried to work on the half-pipe but I got too frustrated so we stopped. Nobody else would speak to Toad; he'd changed too much for them with his shaved head, Docs, and braces. I was the only one left who had anything to do with him and I ended up paying the price for it…

I was going to see this local band called The Warlock Pinchers. They were playing their last show and it was at a club downtown called The 15th. I was meeting Phil and Sarah there because they were going out to dinner or something beforehand.

When going to this club, the only place to park was underneath a viaduct a few blocks away. I didn't mind the walk from my car. I was more used to downtown Denver and wasn't as freaked out walking around at night, even under the aged concrete viaduct.

I was halfway to the club when I thought I heard someone calling to me.

"Hey! Hey, man! What's going on?"

The voice was abrasive. I kept walking until I heard it again closer.

"Hey, dude, slow down. I'm talking to you."

I made the mistake of turning around. Behind me stood four or five guys. All with shaved heads, flight jackets, and blue laces. I knew what that meant. It meant they were Sharps. These were the skinheads who would beat up racist skinheads. They were like rival gangs. I didn't know what they wanted with me but I knew it wasn't good.

"Hey, man, we've seen you around."

"Don't you hang around with that pussy Toad?"

I nodded, and spoke quickly.

"We used to skate together. But I've got nothing to do with what he's doing now. Just someone I used to skate with."

"But you still hang out with him, right?"

I didn't like where this was going. The two outermost guys of the group started moving toward me. I spoke again, this time sounding more desperate.

"I'm not part of his shit, just look at me, man!"

"Yeah, but it's like guilt by association. If you're not doing something about the problem, then you're part of the problem!"

The lead guy took a swing at me. Somehow, I avoided it. But, as I turned, someone punched me hard in the side of the head. I felt my hearing drop out for a second; buzzing followed as I staggered. I punched toward one of them in an effort to make a hole and get away. It was already too late. Wherever I turned someone was in front of me or in back, punching, kicking, or holding me. I fought as hard as I could to keep my hands in front of my face and every time they knocked me to the ground I tried to get up as fast as I could. But it didn't matter. They beat the shit out of me.

The rest was a blur. I remember seeing the viaduct above as I heard them shout things about Toad. I think I might have blacked out because when they were gone and I finally got up from the ground it seemed later. There was no sign of them or anyone else. I was in terrible condition. I limped, trying to make my way up the street toward the club. I was cold and dazed, having trouble feeling my teeth, and something on my face or lip felt torn. There was dirty blood all over my face, in my eyes. Everywhere.

When I got up to the club, people looked at me like I was a leper or something. I just wanted to find Phil—I knew if I could find Phil I could get through this. Phil would get me home.

I was completely out of it and the fucking bouncers wouldn't let me into the club.

"You need to clear out of here!"

"My friend is inside. I need to find my friend."

"You need to go home or something. You're not coming in here."

"You look like a liability!"

"I just need to find my friend, so he can give me a ride."

I continued to plead with them, but they still wouldn't let me in. Not even for a second. I didn't know what I was going to do. I was about to collapse right there on the sidewalk and give up when I heard a familiar voice from the street behind me.

"Hey, man, you okay? Do you need some help or something?"

It was the guy who we'd built the couch cushion fort with at the last Sweater Party. I had never learned his name, but he was there, leaning out of the passenger window of a car. There was a girl behind the wheel.

"Do you need some help, man?"

I nodded as I slumped down onto the concrete steps.

The bouncer raised his voice at me.

"I said you need to get the fuck out of here!"

"The guy's been jumped or something, man. Chill out!"

Before I knew it, I was in the passenger seat of the car. My new friend was inside the club looking for Phil and Sarah. I guess it was his girlfriend's car; she kept asking me if I was okay. I had never met the girl before, and it was embarrassing to have this be our first meeting. Through my swollen lips and a mental haze, I kept telling her how many of them there were. Finally, Phil came rushing out of the club with Sarah right behind.

Phil was beside himself with anger.

"What the fuck! What the fuck! What happened?"

"I got jumped! I was walking to the club… There were four or five of them."

"Were you drunk or something? Why did they jump you?"

Sarah cut in, "Phil! Calm down, Phil!"

"Were they jocks?"

"Sharps, jumped me because of Toad."

Phil went silent. He looked pissed. I could see a million thoughts going through his head.

"Because of Toad... Fucking asshole!"

"Phil, calm down. Right now we need to get him home."

I wasn't used to Sarah being the level-headed one.

They tried to clean my face up with a T-shirt that was in the backseat of the car. Every time Sarah touched my face with the wadded-up shirt it stung. My nose was starting to throb, and everyone in the car thought it was broken—everyone being Phil, Sarah, AJ, and his girlfriend Michelle. They had introduced themselves to Phil and Sarah as they talked about what to do with me.

"I wonder if we should take him to the hospital?" AJ said.

Sarah looked as if she was going to start crying.

"He looks bad, Phil. Maybe we should?"

Phil and I insisted on just getting me home; I didn't want this to be any bigger of a deal than it already was. AJ drove me home in his car, Sarah drove hers, and Phil drove my car behind. I kept drifting in and out on the way home, but I did have the thought that it was a bold move for Phil to drive my car without a license.

I had a black eye for a fucking week. Luckily, I don't think anything was broken that night, maybe my nose a little. But broken or not I was really sore. You could see where a pair of Docs had kicked into my side. I walked with a wincing stagger for a few days because of how sore my ribs were. A year before, people at school would have made fun of me for getting jumped, but now they were asking with concern what happened. It made me mad at all of them. A year ago they would have been happy to see one of the freaks get a beat down.

My mom was really upset. She was almost frantic. She wanted to call the police; she wanted to pack up and move away. I tried to play it cool around her and I insisted that it was a random act and that I was simply in the wrong place at the wrong time. She said I was a walking target because of the way I looked.

"You need to cut your hair and wear some normal clothes. You are constantly a target to these people!"

"This is who I am, I can't change it. I'm not going to try," I said with great frustration.

She looked at me with a kind of remorse. I could tell she wished my father were here to help her deal with the situation. Maybe he would have had some logic about boys, or about growing up and fighting that would have made it all better. Instead, she just had me looking back at her with a black eye and an exasperated look on my face.

When word got to Toad about what happened, he called a couple times to apologize but I wouldn't talk to him. Fuck him. It was his choices that made all of this happen. I don't know how he found out about it, and I didn't care. I guess Rachel called him up and yelled at him.

Time passed. Because of the incident that night, Toad was now completely separated from the rest of us. I could tell he felt really bad. I could see it on his face when I ran into him in the halls at school. But I didn't care; those guys almost killed me because of him. School was now uncomfortable because it was the one place we were all guaranteed to run into each other. A couple of times a fistfight almost broke out between Phil and Toad.

I was more and more freaked out about losing control. Getting jumped made me feel like I had no control, losing my father made me feel like I had no control, my mom spending more time with that guy made me feel like I had no control. I started obsessing over trying to regain control of the things in my life. I stopped drinking completely. No more letting my guard down. My new thing would be no more loss of control. I wouldn't allow myself to open any doors that were holding back the dark shit inside me.

I couldn't help thinking about how much the next school year was going to suck. Rachel and Sarah both would be gone. Since they were a grade above us, this was their last year. Phil was really bummed about it, too. The good news for him was that Sarah was going to school only twenty miles away in Boulder. Rachel was going to school somewhere out on the East Coast. Ironic that her brother went west, and she was going east. It all had to do with acceptance and scholarships, two things I clearly had no comprehension of.

It was the last week of school when the seniors didn't have to come to class anymore that Phil and I realized just how much we were going to miss having the girls around. I could tell Rachel and Sarah were nervous about going off to college themselves. Whenever the subject came up, they wore the same expression that Rob had when he was about to leave for the first time.

We went to Rachel and Sarah's graduation dressed as freaky as possible. It was our way of showing support for the way they really were, not the way they had to look in their caps and gowns. While we were sitting there watching the ceremony, I thought about Elizabeth. I felt like she should be up there standing with the two of them. Where she was now? What was she doing? No one ever heard from her anymore. Just as Phil, Toad, and I had drifted apart, so had the girls.

Soon, none of these concerns would matter. Rob would be back in a few days and there would finally be another Sweater Party. By now the Morrissey reference to the party was forgotten and in the past. Rachel didn't even bother bringing it up herself. We barely had to mention the party to people, and because of the status of Alternative and the popularity it now sadly had, word of the party quickly spread outside of our little circle.

All of the people from Chaos, The 15th, and the Freak Table were fine. But now others were asking about the party—people from school, people in letter jackets, girls who once wore cheerleader outfits. It was just another sad reminder of how things were changing. Having them hate us was bad enough, having them love us may have been worse. I was beginning to understand Gabo's warning that day in the parking lot of the grocery store.

Rachel and I were spending more time together. She seemed to like me a lot more now that I wasn't drunk all the time or hanging out with Toad. Often we were getting coffee downtown or going to see movies or just hanging out with Phil and Sarah.

One night, when Rachel and I were sitting in a café downtown, we got news that Toad and his friends jumped the guys who beat me up. The news made Rachel upset and it didn't make me feel better about any of it. It actually made me more pissed off at Toad.

Everyone went to meet Rob at the airport the afternoon he flew in; well, everyone except for me because I was at my shitty job. I was excited for the party, though. I even placed one of the flyers for it on my bathroom mirror.

It wasn't that I always wanted to be pissed off. It wasn't that I had transformed overnight into some kind of agitated ghoul. I tried to fight it often. I tried to fool myself into thinking I was fine and finished with the grieving. Many times I thought I had put it all behind me. Then I would go through another cycle and suddenly I would be making poor decisions, pissing people off, and alienating myself again.

This would be the last Sweater Party. We all knew it. Rob was already gone, Rachel was leaving, and when they were both in college it was well understood their parents were going to split up. Things were going to change. An era was going to fade away.

We all worried about it, but none of us discussed it. We just wanted to enjoy the party. I couldn't think of a time when we'd all be together again, the main group of us anyway, the ones who met up at the Freak Table.

After I got off work, Phil and I went to Chaos. We passed out flyers to those we knew and wanted to see—people like Steve, Mikey, Gabo, AJ, Tim, and the people from the scene who we trusted.

I only had a few flyers left and was trying to figure out who they should go to when I saw her…Elizabeth.

It was like seeing a ghost, in a way. She still had the look of someone thinking heavy thoughts, a look that I most certainly wore myself these days.

I rushed over to her and told her how good it was to see her. And that everyone wondered how she was doing. She was hesitant. How could she be that way after all this time? I tried not to let it bother me and I told her about Rachel and Sarah's graduation. I then told her Rob was back and that there was going to be one more party. I started to hand her a flyer when I was interrupted.

"What's that?" A grumbling voice made me freeze.

I turned to find one of the skinhead guys hovering over Elizabeth. He put his arm around her.

"Who the fuck are you, and why are you talking to my girlfriend?"

I had to look shocked... She turned to him and spoke, but I couldn't hear what she said.

He looked me up and down with disgust. As he started to step forward, she grabbed his arm.

"He's fine. He's an old friend, it's harmless."

After all of this time, I was once again referred to as harmless. Fuck harmless. Fuck this. This was where she had been all this time? This was why the other girls hadn't heard from her?

"What's that?"

The guy motioned to the flyer in my hand.

I wasn't about to let the last Sweater Party be ruined. I crumpled it in my hand.

"It's nothing, for a show, but you guys wouldn't be into it. It's *punk* rock," I said.

I started to walk away when he grabbed the shoulder of my shirt.

"What's that supposed to mean?"

I looked at him. Then I looked at Elizabeth long and hard. Whatever glow she once had, it was now gone. Whatever energy or spirit I once saw in Elizabeth, I wasn't seeing it anymore.

"I don't like your fucking attitude!" he said.

Elizabeth was starting to look concerned. Just then Toad walked up, getting between us. He patted the large guy on the shoulder.

"He's cool, man, he's cool!"

Toad said some other things that I couldn't make out but they had to do with me getting jumped. The large guy nodded his head, gave me one final scowl, and walked away with Elizabeth. She was too ashamed to even give me an apologetic look as they disappeared into the crowd.

Now it was just Toad and I standing there. If that wasn't awkward enough, Phil had just walked up.

"What the fuck is going on?" Phil asked, while looking at Toad.

Toad looked back. Now they were both sizing each other up. Not a picture any of us would have imagined three years ago.

"It's got nothing to do with him. I just had a run-in with Elizabeth and her *new* boyfriend."

I was so frustrated.

"I don't know why she picks the fucking people she does! She really likes assholes, if you ask me," I grumbled.

She met that guy a couple of weeks after you went to the funeral. I never got a chance to tell you about it, because you won't talk to me anymore, man," said Toad.

"I wonder why that is, Toad!?" Phil barked at him. It started a shouting match between the two.

"What the fuck is wrong with you?"

"What the fuck is wrong with you!"

"Look at yourself, man. What the fuck are you doing?"

"What about you? You and your perfect fucking life! I just have the guts to be what I am!"

"And what's that?"

"Sick of getting kicked around. Now nobody fucks with me!"

"Yeah, well, they still fuck with your *friends*, don't they?"

There was a moment of silence while they both looked at me. This was where I would normally come in and play the mediator. This was where I would jump in and say all the things that needed to be said. I would be witty, and sly, and maybe even a little stylish. I would be eloquent in my choice of words.

"I'm leaving," I said. "Phil, let's go."

I started walking away.

"See you around, Toad," I said.

"So that's it? I just came over here and saved your ass and that's it? Next time I'll remember not to give a shit!"

I turned back around. I think what I said probably did more damage than any punch or kick I could have thrown. I told him the truth.

"You never needed those fucking guys for strength. We would have always had your back, and not for any bullshit reasons. We would have always had your back because you were our friend."

Toad stood there, not knowing what to say.

I walked away.

Phil and I drove in silence half the way home. We passed under streetlights, merged onto highways, and took the exit for our neighborhood before Phil spoke.

"I can't believe Sarah's going off to school," he said as he watched the houses pass by.

"Yeah, but she'll be close enough for us to go hang out with her."

"Yeah, I just hope she doesn't get too busy with her new life there, ya know?"

"Yeah."

"So what was up with Elizabeth? Was she really with that guy?"

"I guess so..."

"Who would have thought, huh?"

When I got home, I placed the cassette for the album *Technique* into my stereo. I fell asleep to it. The lyrics fit the melancholy of my mood perfectly. Tomorrow would be the last Sweater Party.

Chapter 16: The Last Sweater Party

Saturday morning was hard. My mom had decided we had to sell my father's truck so we could keep our own two cars, and be able to keep paying for the insurance. We were selling it to some people who used to work with my dad. I knew that it was for the best and I knew that we needed the money, so I didn't say anything about it. But it bothered me because I knew how much my dad loved that truck. He loved driving it, working on it, and hauling stuff around in it. I was sad to see it go.

It seemed that too often we had to shed the things that linked him to our lives. It was hard to see those people driving the truck away, knowing there would now be nothing more than an oily spot where it used to be parked.

My mom left awhile later, and I once again had the house to myself. I prowled around as I'd been doing whenever she wasn't there, looking through my dad's things. While digging through the garage, I found some white paint, which gave me an idea.

Last Christmas, my mom had given me a black leather motorcycle jacket. I wore it all of the time. I'd even wear it when it was too hot to wear a leather jacket. It was my second skin. It was funny—in some ways, the kind of jacket you wore would dictate where you ended up in the scene. The guys wearing leathers and the guys wearing flights— might as well have called us the Jets and the Sharks, or the Greasers and the Socs.

I had finally broken in the jacket and I wanted to paint something on the back to really make it mine. Everyone had some type of signature to his or her leather. I carefully painted myself a FACT number. Every New Order album I'd seen had one, so I thought it would be cool to have one of my own. On the bottom of the back of the jacket I wrote

FACT 1973. I figured it would make sense to those who knew what it was. I just hoped the paint would dry before the party.

I then went into the bathroom and did my hair up. If this was going to be the last party, I wanted to go out looking good. I skipped the heavy make-up and instead put on a touch of eyeliner. While putting it on, I took a long, cold look into my eyes. Again, it was just me standing there. The house was empty—no family, no Toad, no Phil. Everyone and everything I knew was drifting apart.

Phil showed up later, ready for the party. We walked out into the backyard and sat on the unfinished half-pipe. He drank a beer I'd found him in the fridge, and I had a cup of coffee I had just made. We sat together on that monstrosity and talked about things.

It was a conversation that felt strangely adult. Like a conversation we'd be having in the years to come—not now. Both of us felt anticipation for the party over an undercurrent of worry. I was worried about my future and he was worried about his and Sarah's future.

Once Phil was good and buzzed, we climbed into my car and made the drive from my neighborhood to Rob and Rachel's. The class difference in the neighborhoods seemed to have become more and more noticeable in the past year, especially after having to do things like sell my father's truck. Not that I was bitter toward them. They had their own set of fucked-up problems. But I was really starting to feel the effects of what was happening at my home. Plus I was working now and I knew how hard you had to work for such little money.

Phil and I both agreed that we were happier before cars, bills, colleges, and all of the things that come with being adult. We agreed that we'd been happier when it was just two skateboards, some good sidewalk, and a Friday night ahead of us.

We got to Rob and Rachel's house and I insisted on parking in the driveway.

"I have seniority," I barked at them. "Later, there's gonna be a ton of people here and I want front row parking."

They laughed and agreed. The first thing I did at the party was tell Sarah about my run-in with Elizabeth.

"I guess she's just going through another tough phase right now. Things at home have never been good for her. She doesn't see Rachel and me anymore. Soon we'll be off at different colleges and she'll be stuck here. It can't be easy, I guess."

Sarah didn't sound annoyed. Not as much as she should have been. The girls were so pissed at Toad for getting involved with that crowd, and now they were looking the other way when it came to Elizabeth. Maybe it was because she wasn't really part of their lives anymore? They hadn't heard from her in a long time and they were soon going to be moving on to new places. Maybe they were too busy looking forward to care about what she was doing?

"It's not really her that's the problem. It's that things just drift apart, right?"

I looked at Sarah. She studied me right back. I was just starting to think about how I'd never given her the credit she deserved, when she interrupted my thought.

"As for that guy she's with—I don't even know what to tell you about that."

"Yeah, I really don't care about that," I said. "She should just make it a point not to lose touch with you and Rachel. That's all."

"You're not *into* her anymore?" Sarah asked me. I shook my head no.

"Not for a long time. She's not really the person I thought she was."

"*We* thought you still liked her."

"No."

Suddenly, I realized I didn't want to talk about it anymore.

Which was fine because Sarah was up and gone soon after. She was already across the room talking with Rachel and I was just glad to drop the subject. I walked out back to find Rob listening to AJ and Michelle.

When I joined the conversation, they were on the subject of the *mainstream* people at school.

"Get this. I saw a guy at my school this week wearing a flannel shirt tied around his waist and a fucking letter jacket up top, can you believe that? A flannel and a letter jacket…"

"God, that makes me sick."

The group laughed.

"At our school, the principal made a rule that no one can tuck their Docs into their boots."

"Don't you mean tuck their pants into their Docs?"

"That's what's so funny! The principal doesn't get it. He thinks 'Docs' are 'Docker pants.' So he keeps running around the school saying no one is to tuck their Docs into their boots!"

We roared in laughter. All except Rob—he smiled as if it were only slightly amusing.

Rob changed the subject and began telling us how many places near his college you could find good music or clothing. He also talked about one of his professors, who was a famous alternative filmmaker or something.

The party seemed a little empty without Toad there showing off. It also seemed odd knowing that Elizabeth wouldn't be showing up. Rachel and I talked about it for a bit. She was much more disappointed with Elizabeth than Sarah was.

"Well, I think she's trying to do this thing where she associates us with being part of her past, when she can be just as much a part of our future. Rob left for school, we still keep in touch with him, he still comes back. I don't see why it would be any different for Sarah and me? Besides, Sarah's not even really leaving. Beth could see her any time she wanted."

"Yeah, maybe she's annoyed because you guys are going off to real colleges and everything?"

"Well, she shouldn't be. I even tried to get her to apply to the same school I'm going to. She just shrugged it off and said something about art school or something."

Rachel seemed to be glowing that night. I was glad that she was having a good time. Whenever Rob was back she was happier, and I was sure she was happy to be out of high school. I knew I'd miss seeing her when she was off at college.

The party got crowded almost instantly. All kinds of people we did and didn't know were showing up. Unfortunately, people from our school were showing up in herds. These people now wanted to hang out with us? They wanted to drink with us and listen to what we were listening to? Most of the people at the party didn't mind, but I couldn't help holding a grudge. They had made our lives hell for too long. I wasn't going to just drop it.

I couldn't help but roll my eyes when some cheerleader girls from school showed up. These were the same girls who watched Brad and his friends ridicule me time and time again… Rob took me aside when he saw my look of disgust.

"Dude, you gotta chill out. You're going to get out of that damn school, move on, and realize that all of this is bullshit anyway. Don't let them get to you."

I nodded like I understood him, and maybe deep down I even knew he was right, but I couldn't help feeling the anger.

Before I could argue with him about the way things were, Rob gave me forty bucks and asked if I'd run to the store and get some more chips and snack food. Being the only sober one at the party sucked when errands needed to be run. I guess I didn't mind, seeing as how I wanted to get away from some of those people anyway. Rachel came along and we ended up having a great time at the store.

We spent half an hour in the cereal aisle looking for what box of cereal had the best prize in it.

"You know, the toys you could get when we were kids were way better than what you get now. Kids today are getting ripped off with their cereal prizes."

After our discussion on cereal box prizes, Rachel asked me more about my run-in with Elizabeth the night before. I told her pretty much the same thing I'd told Sarah and then I changed the subject as quickly as possible. And then for old time's sake, I grabbed a couple two-liter bottles of generic orange soda.

I snuck a box of Captain Crunch with Crunch Berries into all of the stuff we were picking up for Rob. Rachel and I decided that later we'd dig through the box and claim the prize for ourselves.

We weren't gone long, but by the time we got back the place had blown up into a full raging house party. It looked like a scene from a bad '80s teen movie. There were cars everywhere and the front was crowded with people smoking and hanging out.

The music coming from inside the house was loud enough to hear on the street. It was crazy. Rachel headed straight into the chaos to do damage control.

When we got inside she was pissed off because some guy none of us knew was playing some kind of rap-rock on her stereo.

"Oh no! No way, that is not being played in my house! Not my party!"

She yanked the CD from the stereo, ranting to herself about Morrissey, Sweater Parties, and The Smiths.

I laughed when she asked him if he even knew what kind of party he was at. When he shrugged, saying, "No," she actually led him outside like a schoolteacher disciplining a child.

"You'll have to drink in the backyard if you want to stay," she told him.

I couldn't help cracking up. I couldn't remember the last time I'd laughed like that. I couldn't remember the last time I'd really laughed. It felt good.

As Rachel came back inside, someone put a tape they had bought at a warehouse party into the stereo. They said it was rave. The music was completely electronic, but not like the industrial I was so used to. There were no spaces between the tracks and most of the songs didn't have any lyrics. Someone else sitting in the living room referred to it as techno as I studied the case for the cassette

There were too many people at the party and more were showing up. Even though I was glad to find some friends from Chaos and The 15th, there were too many bastards from my school showing up. Everyone except for me was having a great time. I felt like the vultures from our school were picking at the corpse of our scene.

I decided it would be a good time for me to escape. It was getting late and the party wasn't any closer to winding down, and it was just a matter of time till the cops showed up. I was certain Rob and Rachel must have paid off the neighbors to keep the noise complaints down.

I grabbed the box of cereal and decided to go wander out to the soccer fields behind the house. That was where the real magic was, that was where those clear, untouched memories existed. I looked around for a small group to take with me. I talked to AJ and his girlfriend, but they were about to leave for the night, so they were out. I tried to get Phil to go, but he was consumed with talking to the guy who brought the techno tape. There was nobody to venture out with. I was even starting to wish Toad was around. He would have gone, at least the Toad I used to know would have.

I sat watching the busy room in front of me. In a way, most of the people were strangers.

Fuck it. I'll just go out there myself. As I prepared to walk out the door, I felt someone behind me. It was Rachel.

"Did you want to get out of here for a while? All these people are getting to me."

She was reading my mind. She waved goodbye to Sarah and we were out the door. We didn't climb the fence like the times before. We walked through the neighborhood to the entrance of the Vita-Course. Rachel kept insisting that she was wearing a skirt and didn't want to climb the fence, and wanted for once to behave like a young lady. She was joking of course, because she was always the most lady-like of all my friends.

The noise of the party faded as we continued walking through the neighborhood. I had the box of cereal under my arm and she carried a bottle of wine. When we got to the opening of the soccer fields, I was hit with a wave of shock. It looked like we had just walked up to a disaster site. Where the soccer fields once were, where we had come of age, was gone. It was all gone.

Everything had been plowed over into dirt. The area had been stripped. Markers holding orange fluorescent fabrics stuck up eerily from the ground. Large earth-moving vehicles stood silently in the distance. The Vita-Course was gone, the soccer fields, all of it…gone. The only things remaining were mountains of dirt.

They were probably building apartments or a mini mall or something painfully un-special. The wave of disappointment rushed through me—I had just lost another friend. Just like my father, just like Elizabeth or Toad, it was all gone.

"When did they start doing this?" Rachel asked herself aloud.

She looked around in disbelief. I looked around. It was empty. The bent goal post, the grass, the jogging course—it was decimated.

We didn't know what else to do, so we just started walking toward the hills of dirt.

"This is really freaking me out," Rachel said as she continued to gaze around at the absence.

We climbed to the top of one of the dirt-clod hills and sat down.

"I guess this isn't too lady-like, is it?"

She was joking out of her own discomfort.

"Do you think things are gonna change between Phil and Sarah when she leaves?" Rachel asked me.

"I don't know. In some ways it's probably more up to Sarah than Phil. She's going to be surrounded by all these new things, new places, new guys, you know…"

"Yeah, I think Phil is always gonna be Phil. He's very loyal to her." she said.

"Time will tell, right? Isn't that what they say?" I was trying to be clever again.

"Yeah."

We interrupted ourselves to talk about our box of cereal and our favorite Saturday morning cartoons. Despite the sadness of the Vita-Course being gone, Rachel and I were enjoying each other's company.

We took turns throwing dirt-clods at a port-a-pot that was sitting in the distance. We laughed about how funny it would be if someone were in there while we were doing so.

In the black of night, on that big pile of dirt, I felt incapable of recapturing the epic feelings I'd once had out there. I didn't think I would ever be capable of anything epic again. Just as I was going to suggest that we go back to the party, something happened.

I'm not sure what we were talking about, but suddenly Rachel leaned over and kissed me. I was surprised for a moment but I didn't pull away or anything. It felt right. Nothing had felt right for so long… I leaned forward and kissed her back. She looked so different this close, her brown eyes wide.

"How did we end up here?" I asked.

Instantly I wished I would have kept my big mouth shut. I didn't need to know, it didn't matter, because it was right. Just as I was starting to fill with dread, she spoke in the softest voice.

"I've liked you for a really long time. More than friends like each other. I'll be leaving soon… It would be a shame if we didn't have a kiss."

I smiled as I looked off at the construction vehicles in the distance. I didn't know what to say.

"Sarah told me what you said about Elizabeth, about how you weren't into her anymore… I was always intimidated by that, I guess…"

I didn't know what to say back to her. Instead, I took her hand and held it in mine. She smiled and pulled herself closer to me. I put my arm around her and held her close to me. Maybe just this once, I didn't need to say anything.

We held hands the entire way back to the house.

"I can't believe they plowed up the Vita-Course!"

"Yeah, I can't believe it's gone!"

We got back to the party, which was still crazy. Rachel took my hand and led me through all the people and up the stairs. We got to the door I knew opened to her bedroom. She cracked it open, looking inside. She then turned around smiling.

"I didn't clean my room. I didn't think anyone would be up here tonight. I just have to make sure it's not too messy."

She crept into her room then opened the door again, pulling me inside. As soon I was in the room, I saw the mirror. Instantly drawn to it, I walked over to look at the pictures on it. This time, as I looked at all the images, I noticed something had changed.

Pictures including me had somehow made their way onto the mirror. I wasn't alone; I was there with them, with her. It was a map illustrating the last few years, showing the paths we had all tread.

I turned to find Rachel sitting on the bed, looking up at me, absolutely beautiful. The room was soft, like a painting or something, but I was really there. I was part of the image now. I didn't think my life still would have moments like this, moments that made everything better.

The bedroom door suddenly burst open with a crash as Sarah rushed in. I could hear shouting downstairs and there were tears in her eyes.

"Toad just showed up. He and Phil are yelling, I think they're going to fight!"

I took off running. I had no idea what I'd do when I got to them.

As I got downstairs, there was an opening in the crowd as people moved to get away from them. Toad and Phil's arms were locked, grabbing onto one another while they tossed around the room. They were still shouting at each other.

As I got closer, someone grabbed me. It was some kid I didn't know.

"You shouldn't get involved, man!"

Who the fuck did he think he was? I shoved him hard out of my way. He flew back into the crowd

Before I could get to Phil and Toad, they were throwing punches. It was a full-fledged fistfight right in the middle of Rob and Rachel's house. Phil was holding his own with Toad… I was impressed. He was no longer the skittish kid in a Dead Kennedy's shirt he'd been when we met. As I tried to get in the middle of them to break it up, I could tell Toad was loaded drunk. All I could see was a frantic blur as I tried to pry them off each other. Rob joined in, too. He managed to pull Phil away as I struggled to hold Toad back. I caught one of Toad's elbows right in the face.

Rob was shouting at Phil to calm down. I could also hear Sarah screaming for it to stop. I saw the faces of all the people at the party, these strangers, watching us in horror and delight.

With great effort, we dragged them outside. It was hectic and there were cheers and more shouting as we made it outside.

I had never seen Rob that pissed.

"I come back from school and find you guys still acting like fucking kids! You're just little fucking kids, when are you going to grow the fuck up? When are you going to let this shit go?"

I felt like he was yelling at all of us.

"You haven't been around! You haven't seen how everything is now!" Phil shouted back while pointing at Toad.

Toad was now sitting on the ground, drunk and about to break down. He was desperate. He couldn't have been farther from the intimidating guy I'd met at that small, stained lunch table a few years before.

What happened to us? We were just kids in the fucking suburbs… How could our lives be like this?

I looked over at Phil, who was finally starting to settle down. Rob stood there shaking his head in disgust. He looked like someone's father.

I laughed out loud.

"What's so funny?" he barked.

"Don't give me that look! I wasn't the one fighting in your living room!" I said, continuing to laugh.

I couldn't help it. I couldn't help but laugh at how absurd everything had become. Rob glared at me, sizing me up. The age difference between us never felt so big. Then he cracked a smirk.

"Things get better, you assholes, I swear things get better! I just want you to get there in one piece."

Toad looked up. He was a shell of who he used to be. I wondered if I looked as tired and used up. Sarah, Rachel, and a few others were silently watching us from the porch. I looked back at Toad, who was sitting on the ground falling to pieces. Tears were welling in his eyes. I felt that he didn't need to be seen like this.

"I'm gonna take Toad and sober him up."

I didn't know what else to do so I reached toward Phil to shake his hand. He looked over at Toad, his face now filled with pity. Phil shook my hand.

I looked back over at Rachel. Moments ago it had been just she and I, nothing else mattered. We were in her room, there was magic… And now I had to leave with Toad. I had to leave because it was the right thing to do. From the look on her face I think she knew it was the right thing to do, too.

I helped Toad into my car. As we drove away, all I could think about was how much I didn't want to leave. More than anything I didn't want to leave this last party. I didn't want to leave Rachel.

I had to dodge Toad's puke as we climbed the ladder to the roof. Maybe in the condition he was in, it wasn't the best idea to climb up to the roof of the grocery store, but I didn't know where else to take him.

We sat up on that roof for a long time. Toad chewed meekly on Cheetos and drank some 7-Eleven coffee. It had to be a hell of a combination, but I was just relieved he was eating anything that might sober him up.

The night felt still and dark as Toad spoke.

"I'm just not happy anymore, you know?"

I don't know why he hadn't been able to admit that to me before, but I guess he hadn't been able to admit it to *himself.*

Toad stared into the distance. I wondered if he saw the same things out there that we used to see. I didn't mean the dark neighborhoods or the twinkling orange streetlights. I wondered if he saw any kind of future, any of the limitless possibilities. I know I sure didn't see them anymore when I looked out there. My horizon had changed. So had his.

"If you're not happy with the life you have, maybe you should change it."

Great advice. Easy to say to someone, but hard to listen to or follow myself.

"I just thought things would be different, man. I thought things would get easier. When you're a kid and you got no power to change things, it sucks, you know? But now we're a little older, and we still can't make things any better…"

Toad stopped himself. He raised his eyebrows and shrugged. He knew that I knew exactly what he was talking about. I might have been the only one in Toad's life who knew what he meant.

As we sat there looking out over suburbia and talking, the sky was starting to lighten to a dark shade of blue. It was a warning that daytime was soon to come. We agreed it best to get down from the roof before people could see us.

It seemed the Sweater Parties never finished the way I thought they would. Who would have known we'd end up wherever we did at the end of the night? This was far better than where I ended up after the last party, but it wasn't the magic I was hoping to recapture.

After I dropped off Toad, I drove home in the early morning light. I thought about Rachel, the walk we had, the kiss, and I wondered what would have happened if Toad hadn't show up and gotten in the fight with Phil.

Rachel wasn't mad that I had to leave the last Sweater Party. In fact, she told me that I did the right thing, as she often thought I did. It was nice having someone tell me I was doing the right thing after an entire year where people acted like I was only capable of doing wrong.

That summer, for three very short months, Rachel and I were together as a couple. It was great; she was the closest thing I had to a normal high school girlfriend. We both knew it wouldn't last because she was going off to school, but it didn't matter. We'd get coffee, go to movies, or sometimes just sit around together. Those few months with her had a kind of healing effect on me.

There would always be a place inside me that lamented not getting approval from Elizabeth, not getting a return on the affection I had for her. But, now it didn't matter. Now I cared very much for Rachel in a different way, and it made me feel better about everything else.

In those three months, I also grew closer to Rob. He had become an even better friend than before. He felt comfortable enough to admit to me that when he left for college he came out of the closet. He had admitted to himself and his family he was gay. And that summer, he felt comfortable admitting it to me. He said he had known for years, but didn't want to face it until he got out of our high school.

It's strange. I had spent almost my entire high school experience doing what I could to *not* fit in. He spent his entire time hiding the fact that he didn't. Maybe it was smart of him, I don't know. If I went through the hell I did just for being a skater, who knew what they would have done to him?

I could tell things would never be the same between Phil and Toad, but at least after that night they weren't bitter enemies. They could at least respect that they used to be friends. Toad did start making some changes. He really got back into music. He discovered all kinds of important bands like Social Distortion, Fugazi, and Rollins Band. His appearance started changing, his hair started growing out, and before we knew it he was back to normal. Well, as normal as you could be for someone named Toad.

Chapter 17: The Fast Summer

Before I knew it, the fast summer was over. Rachel was leaving for college. Phil, Sarah, and I went to the airport to send her off. For the first time since I met her, Rachel looked scared. Not like the kind of scared she was when I fought Brad Thompson in her front yard, or the kind of scared she was when she admitted she liked me for the first time—this was something daunting, something different. She was moving off to a new place all alone. I knew she'd be okay and I hoped in a couple weeks she would know it, too.

We hugged each other long and hard at the airport that day. Holding onto each other, we promised to keep in touch and never forget the last few months. And then she was gone.

The others were also gone now. Rob had left a few days earlier, and Sarah had already moved onto her campus in Boulder.

Phil, Toad, and I would have a very different school year ahead of us. We didn't know how or what would change, but we knew it would. Everything was always changing around us. The one constant was the Sweater Party, and now even it was gone. It was part of a past that many would never know or understand.

The night before my senior year began, I drove over to Rachel and Rob's house. I didn't go in. I didn't even step into the front yard. I just sat there in the street, leaning up against my car, staring at the house in front of me.

It was dark and silent. Without the party, the people, or the life I once knew inside, it was just this big empty house. The windows were as dark and uncertain as the future in front of me.

I thought about all that had happened inside those walls. We entered those parties as kids wanting to be adults. Now we were closer to adults wanting to go back to being kids.

I thought about Rachel, wondering where she was, and if she was happy. I thought about Rob and Sarah and their college lives. And then I thought about Elizabeth.

The girl who was most likely not off at some kind of college, the girl who, much like me, was nowhere close to that happily ever after just yet. I hoped wherever she was that she was happier than when I knew her.

I thought about Toad and Phil. I hoped that as we moved into the year ahead, they would maybe become friends again, and that Toad would find whatever it was he was looking for.

As for me… I thought about those nights with the others, under the stars, laughing and living innocently. I hoped and prayed for more of those nights that lasted forever.